The youngest of four children, born and raised in Godalming, Surrey, Zara took on her first job at fourteen, studied hard and gained a place at Charterhouse. Having taken a year out in Uganda, she went on to read art history at Aberdeen University, graduating in 1994. She has worked in various positions, from Sotheby's, London to the polo grounds of New Zealand. Following an assortment of travels and eye-opening experiences across the globe she settled into nursing.

Married to James who whilst pursuing his own vocation also supports Zara on her final career path of writing. Together they care for their four young children at their home in Godalming, which they share with their dog and cat.

HOME

Zara Howard

HOME

AUSTIN MACAULEY

A CIP catalogue record for this title is
available from the British Library.

ISBN 978 1 905609 35 2

www.austinmacauley.com

First Published (2008)
Austin & Macauley Publishers Ltd.
25 Canada Square
Canary Wharf
London
E14 5L

Printed & Bound in Great Britain

DEDICATION

For my husband, James.

ACKNOWLEDGEMENTS

Thank you to Sarah Hughes for IT support, and to my husband, James, for his support in general.

BELINDI

There were times when she simply couldn't understand how she had come to be somewhere, but knew she had been there all the same. There was a wedding party, being held somewhere, and as ever the journey took hours. Again, as usual, or standard anyway, it was on the back of a Toyota pick-up to get there. She always had these mixed emotions as to whether to be a Westerner or adopt a 'when in Rome' approach. At the wedding party, there was no difference there either. She attempted to join in with the traditional Belindan dancing, though if she adopted her own moves, she was greeted with the same spontaneous applause and laughter.

She admired their spirit, their humour and felt intrigued as to the complete contrast of men to women. The men generally seemed of a slighter build, much slimmer. This was more noticeable because the women were often rather large. This she understood to be compounded by not only tradition in so much as that was the way the men liked their women folk to be, but the way HIV appeared to affect the males. So she learnt it was referred to as 'slim disease'.

There were many stories she heard whilst out there, connected with HIV and AIDS, among them of babies being assaulted by male victims of the disease. In a belief system that, tainted by this terrifying plague, will clutch desperately and with horrifying repercussions to a potential remedy, or cure.

Later, after she had travelled back to England, she found a natural and understandable interest in news reports based on Belindi. One story told of a woman, in the guise of a witch, who was persuading victims of this same disease to wash in a mud pool. This she claimed had magic healing properties. In some ways she was on the right track. It was more the belief that she was taking money or goods or both from these people who she knew would have less than nothing in the first place. On top of this, they were to all intents and purposes, dying.

At the wedding, as she suspected, the women were wearing their traditional dresses, with the squared off, pointy and puffed out shoulders. She could definitely make a parallel with the power dressing 80s style which had become so popular back home with businesswomen. Again, their partners, husbands and so on, wore dark sombre colours, as if they had walked straight off the farm to this wedding, and the women straight from a boutique. For her, they were surreal. She had become strikingly aware of the utter poverty and pestilence around her and yet the women somehow managed to find the money and the time to dress in this finery. The colours were not dissimilar to the sort of outfit a geisha girl might wear; satin or imitation silk materials of turquoise, violet and mandarin. Then there were their hairstyles. She had spoken with one of the teachers at the school where she worked a number of times. She was the Headmaster's secretary and she assumed she had a standard to uphold in her appearance. She had noticed what appeared as a chemical burn on the back of her neck, at the nape and rising up into her hairline. The story was she had gone for a perm and the acids in the hair solution had caused the damaged. Apparently, it was commonplace, not just the suffering which it seemed had to be endured as a matter of course, but the efforts and lengths many women, especially the more educated ones were going, to achieve that western image, the same she had travelled so far from. There was certainly some irony there, surely the more intelligent women could see, could realise this was an unnecessary process to put themselves through?

She had witnessed many times whilst being driven through the capital, Mutabi, the women of all ages working on the roadside. They were bent double, with tools that had seen better days. She didn't know why or how they came to be there half of the time. Perhaps the Government was paying them, to keep the area clear of weeds? More likely, it was common land, which they had grabbed a stake hold of, to try to grow some vegetable or other, or start a banana plantation.

The average diet was pretty sparse, cooking bananas or Matoke, as it was called, maize, jug-fruit, passion fruit, oranges and sweet potatoes would supplement the otherwise bland chicken or goat recipes, put together by the women folk naturally. Whilst the women worked in the kitchen, raised the children and toiled the land, the men drove, either the obligatory imports, Toyota Land Cruiser or pick-up or big delivery trucks. When they weren't driving from one town to the next, they were shacked up with whichever women would put up with them. Into the process, alarmingly, the women, who showed no initial signs or symptoms of the disease, were passing on the HIV virus, worse still, knowingly. Their attitude was that if they were affected they would do their damnedest to take as many poor souls with them as time would allow.

She sometimes felt quite baffled as to quite how corrupt this country was, how utterly desperate. What difference was she making and at the same time, in spite of the job offers of work as a teacher in a new school, she knew she had to take care of herself and her future if she was to have any hope of a real future and a long one at that, God willing. That meant, in all honesty, to pursue securing a place at university in England and getting work with a reputable company. With any luck, where corruption was punished appropriately, or just wouldn't arise in the first place. She felt self-centred, but her saving grace was her understanding or at least the realisation of how things stood in Belindi. You couldn't help the people when bribery and corruption ran so deep it affected the legal system. How could anyone possibly be brought to justice when justice wasn't just in the first place? She did what she could.

There was a distinct moment at the wedding party when it dawned on her the villagers had found a bed for her and carried the thing down to the setting where she was. Almost to her horror, it was a real bed, not a mat on the floor, or some straw, but a huge double bed with a headboard and mattress. It looked so out of place there. She knew enough by now not to offend their hospitality and generosity.

There was a time when she visited a family who knew no English, yet made themselves clear with gestures that they wanted her to have some of their cows' milk. They were virtually insisting. It turned out, they would normally sell every last drop of milk they produced and drink none for themselves. Because they had never seen a Jamambu or white female European, it was an honour to them. She felt the honour was all hers and couldn't get her head around the way she was greeted almost like royalty. An eighteen year old, straight out of school, who only months before had been suspended for staying out too late.

As a compromise, since she was insisting on the wedding guests having the bed for themselves and was getting nowhere fast, she persuaded them to agree to share the bed with her. What with the language barrier and major cultural difference she suddenly found herself in bed with twenty women and children, minimum. Some snored, some looked like they hadn't a care in the world and the whole place swarming with creatures of the night, spiders, beetles and an odour of homemade banana beer, cheap gin and sweat.

Since arriving in Belindi she had noticed immediately a sense of acceptance. The people who picked her up from the airport turned out to be the Brothers who helped run and govern the school, where she was to take up her post as English teacher. As her time there went on, she somehow found herself becoming a part of the community. She would take herself off on quiet afternoons, when the lessons had finished for the day. Then she would walk the dusty, sandy track that led up to the Brothers' residence. As with all buildings in Belindi, it was crumbling in parts, the masonry in need of repair, undoubtedly around the porch and evident on the steps leading up to the veranda. She had lived there long enough to know there was no money to pay anyone skilled enough to put the problems rights. Even if there was they might be corrupt already and demand to be paid double or worse. So she took the same walk by herself and entered the house in her quiet way. Often she heard voices from inside or out in the grounds, but no one ever came to the place where she would always be found, in the music room.

The music room had four stone walls, all whitewashed as was every building here on the school compound. There was a large rectangular opening for a window in front of her and before her a piano. She had taken up piano lessons for a short while, whilst at school, and thought she at least had some appreciation for this beautiful instrument. Amazingly all the keys were in place and after some time, when it had become quite commonplace for her to be in that room, sat on the stool, fingers poised, the notes even sounded reasonably tuned. It irritated her, though, that once she had practised her scales, or at least those she had been taught and knew she had remembered correctly, she would begin to play the two or three tunes she felt confident to perform and that was that. If someone in the house or nearby had been listening and they wanted to comment, pass judgement, give some appraisal or practical criticism or something, she felt fairly confident she could hold her hand up, as well as her head. But the pieces weren't complete and she was sure there must be a few notes that were meant to be majors not minors. The other thing was, could she be boring the people or worse, irritating the people about her with her constant and repetitive noise? She decided to do her own thing. Eventually, really she was past caring. Here she could be her own person, she could experiment, make her own mistakes. She began to play any note her fingers chose to land on! She tried not to think at all. This was real freedom. She tried to put away the structure and purpose of the lessons she had received and just strike the keys for the sheer beauty of the sound they produced individually. Gradually, she would allow her fingers, her arms, her body to run away by themselves. She joked with herself that perhaps she was the undiscovered talent no one had yet heard of – not even herself! Once in a while, when she sat there, she would allow herself to look away from the keys. They only bound her to the path the music teacher would have wanted her to stay true to. She would look out through that white stone window, way across to the school pond, where everyone and everything, from schoolboy, to pick-up, to cattle could be found there, washing, drinking, swimming and beyond to the only main road that led from there out to the towns. With her mind and thoughts away in the distance, her hands took on a life by themselves. She thought to herself, that any minute they would perform a true marvel, a piece of music akin to Mozart or Beethoven, or better than all of them. In truth, nothing more than the odd good note or three would raise her spirits and lift her teenage confidence. That was all this really amounted to anyway, a teenager in angst.

The school pond lay to one side of the compound, visible past some trees to the left, as you approached the school along the drive. One day a neighbouring school paid a visit. The reason being, something to do with a geography exhibition the schools had jointly contributed to. She recalled feeling baffled initially that in a place so run-down, war torn and destitute, some of the people, children even, were still, apparently so utterly confident in their future. They had organised and were carrying off something as commendable and informative as a school exhibition. She didn't get the opportunity to see the work, sadly, but spent some time down at the pond with some of the pupils and the odd member of staff. She chatted amongst her colleagues, sometimes about England but was never as talkative as she was used to. That wasn't the way here, a quiet respectable and respectful manner was the right way to be, she had learnt. Several of the boys were clambering up onto a rock face that seemed to have sprung up out of the dry, gritty earth about it, jutting half out like an army sergeant major standing to attention. The boys were mixing with each other. They were jostling for a space on the rocky diving board to charge off, arms flaying either side of them and collapsing in some unattractive heap into the ripples below. Some oxen had been brought down from the farmstead. This lay to one side of the Brothers' residence. They needed a drink and seemed well used to sharing the water with all and sundry. This included the schools transport that was there at the bank being cleaned by some of the local boys. She wasn't there when it happened. Not that she could have made any difference. Anyway, everyone seemed so protective of her, most of the time. The sight of seeing something as horrible as a drowning, well, maybe they would have decided to send her packing back to that safe haven they call western civilisation. There, naturally, tragedies rarely occur because everyone has been made so aware of the dangers of water. We all get into a panic and drag our children to the nearest pool to drum the necessities into them, every weekend we get the opportunity and the drive. Besides, we Westerners have lifeguards and such people as first aiders, medics and countless health and safety remits to potentially cover everyone's back. For this poor soul, living here, where there was neither the opportunity nor the understanding to be safe in water, had culminated in him going missing and then everyone else waiting for him to re-emerge.

She waited with them. Waited under the pathetic shade of a tree. It had dried up to the point of looking quite ridiculous in an otherwise lush backdrop. There were no leaves to shield itself, nor her from that searing heat. It roasted her as if she might as well have climbed in the oven itself.

Later, she remembered actually saying a prayer of thanks to God, for not leaving her with big, ugly, circular scars on her cheeks. She had plastered every cream, lotion and potion going for days, weeks, to be certain she wasn't going to pay too high a price for her ignorance with regard to the climate out there. The result being that she would resemble a doll.

They said they would have to wait it out, in a vigil almost, that was until the boy's body floated to the surface. She was absolutely disgusted and altogether horrified that the boys were still larking around on the banks, on the rock. They were all splashing each other in that dark, torturous water. She knew it could not have been a worse place to find yourself out of your depth. If the boy had been local and not known how to swim, which amazingly to her, apparently many of the others didn't either, he would have gone down in the company of whatever the cattle chose to leave in there. This would be mixed with countless diseases and chemicals from the dilapidated hulk of the school truck.

Someone took her aside and explained the ritual or folklore. They had to wait for the body to come up, somehow and then each person in turn had to come and look at the recovered body. Look straight at the face, into the place where the eyes would have been. Of course, it hadn't occurred to her that being under the water that long, the fish and God knows what else was in there with him, would have eaten the delicacies that we refer to as the eyes and lips. It made her think, if there was any

20

spirit left in him, that merciless pit hadn't allowed him to either see it, or if it had, he would not really be able to speak of it. She pondered as to why the body must be observed in this way. They told her if it wasn't then that person must be held responsible for the death. The sun had probably got to her a little, or a lot, because she didn't once think that they might either expect her to join in with the custom, as she had apparently been willing to since her arrival. Nor that if she refused, God forbid, that they might accuse her. When one of the teachers reassured her, she would not be expected to walk by the body, she immediately gathered her senses. She understood exactly the situation and her difficult position. Then immediately felt grateful that she had been excused, let off the hook, if you like. How revolting was she. How could she be so self-absorbed, when this child, perhaps only five years her junior, had just lost his life like that. She gathered herself once more. No, that was fair enough. She did feel sorry for the child, but here you had to think about the repercussions of your actions. For a white girl, the only one around she understood for at least one hundred plus kilometres, if she had refused, Christ, bolted even, at the very suggestion of staring into the face of death, death half eaten away by frenzied parasites that infested the waters there, infiltrating into the boy's very skin, his skull. What might have they done? No, customs ran terrifyingly deep out here, how could she be sure they wouldn't blame her? She would learn from this and would be careful. Friendly and cautious always.

As expected, one way or another the boy's body arose and in their customary way, everyone except her, did their bidding and that seemed to be the end of it. There didn't appear to be any investigation, but then why should she be told of any details like that? There was always something going on amongst the people, life went on, or didn't in some cases, and she sort of moved along with it.

She remembered one of many other occasions when her eyes were opened still further to how painfully different her life was to theirs here. After the school holidays, which she had spent lodging at the compound, she wondered as to the whereabouts of several of her class. As big as it was in numbers, at least she had managed to learn many of the faces, if not so successful with their names. Shockingly, two had died from malaria and another had typhoid. Clearly, she had not prepared herself for what was in all honesty, life in this developing country. Their life as the people who belonged here knew it. There were certainly clear and present dangers in the air, in the water they drank, amongst the very people themselves. What she did know was that once they had something as life threatening as these illnesses, they would need to pray. Pray that their family and friends had the required amount to bribe and pay the necessary officials to give them any assistance they could get. Often that would never be enough. She would eventually come to understand that here at least things were rarely as they seemed outwardly. Even if a man could receive all the treatment he needed to rid him of tuberculosis, this was not to say it would double up as a cure-all for the virus that was underlying the condition from the onset, of HIV.

At the school at least, here an employee under the protection of the Brotherhood and being of western origin, she didn't worry herself unduly when she too became ill. There was a school nurse on site and later in another life, many years on, she believed that incredible woman to be largely responsible for her certainty in following her chosen vocation of nursing. She was a pretty and petite lady, very respectable to everyone. You would struggle to get a laugh out of her, but she seemed to smile constantly. With all the disease and illness about her, she felt truly embarrassed to go pestering this woman when she was only constipated. She complained of other symptoms too though, of nausea, but really she just wanted a good laxative, she thought. Since that simple remedy didn't seem to be forthcoming she believed the best thing would be to stay clear of food for the time being and just drink in an effort to undo what the staple diet had allegedly done. Ironic, when she largely only had access to fruit and vegetables anyway.

The hospital she arrived at, naturally, on the back of the obligatory school pick-up, was up a large dust bowl of a hill, way, way off from the school. The very first thing she witnessed was a man arriving in a matching truck next to theirs. He was lying on a sodden mattress on the floor of the truck, with many, many people around him, men and women. The men were calling for help from the doctors and other medical staff. They all helped to raise the man and the mattress off and on to what appeared to be a stretcher of sorts. The women were waving their heads and their hands about. They were shouting and screaming, wailing into the air in their mother tongue. She saw the blood. At first it was there on his shoulder. It had seeped through from his skin beneath his shirt. Then, as the mattress wobbled around, like some sick fairground ride, she saw it beneath him too.

He had been shot she was told. Some of the army men had come to his home, demanding everything and anything. This man, supposedly, had attempted to protect his property and heaven forbid, he had stood up to them.

She couldn't really take it all in but she was feeling so much a part of these people that very quickly she had dismissed this naïve notion and was joining in with the masses in the way she felt she dealt with these things best, a silence which she meant to signify camaraderie.

There were times when she would have liked a little more communication from some of these people, though. Particularly when she was by all accounts being prepped for theatre and had no clue as to why. A nurse had simply entered her room with nothing more than a blade and shaved her in readiness for an internal. After a number of apologetic nicks and cuts, which she felt too dazed and confused to ever be concerned about, in light of the fact this was a country where HIV was rife, she was wheeled down a brightly lit corridor into an even brighter theatre, then darkness.

To this day she is unable to make any sense of why she was in that hospital initially based on the facts. That the hospital staff had informed her, on the one hand, she was in danger of developing an ulcer and yet their internal examinations were done vaginally. To confuse her further, a letter from the hospital, discovered whilst in transit to university in Scotland, revealed she had, and hence was being treated for, malaria. Well, at least that was a claim to fame. Coupled with the belief she was not a hypochondriac after all. That was surely a good enough reason to virtually flea from the country. Once the medical team had confessed they lacked the necessary drugs anyhow.

The patients she left behind at that pathetic place would remain in her memory as utter hopeless causes. She could not recall such horror and affliction of this magnitude. Nothing she might have read about or heard could have prepared her for this. It wasn't that the hospital was badly organised. No doubt it could have used a staff increase, not to say a cash boost. It was the severity of the cases they cared for. She remembered a woman in a wheelchair, which in itself looked archaic. The woman was being pushed about the hospital gardens, which at some point took the wheelchair past the room where she slept on the ground floor. A man was pushing the woman, perhaps an uncle, he looked quite elderly next to her. Although it was difficult to tell with half of her face burnt away. Her forearms had suffered too. She could recollect being informed it was reasonably commonplace in a domestic squabble, for a man to take a kerosene lamp and to hurl the thing alight at his wife. She had tried to grasp the sheer anger, the explosive lamp mimicking the explosive aggressor. Could it have been that he had come home, following many tireless hours on the road? Driving up and down the country's highways for precious little thanks. Only to learn his wife had been unfaithful with some other loser. Or, was it the wife who had kept to her vows. Had she waited for the return of her true love? Was she diligently keeping house for him? Welcoming him home and into her bed yet unknowingly inviting a deadly virus in with him, one that he had conscientiously picked up en route? Either way, this was the thanks she got. The woman's pain and the rivulets of skin, coupled with the legacy of the lamp, travelled across her right cheek, before dribbling over her jaw to her collarbone. She could just make out what must have been an eye on the same side of the face. Whether or not there was still any sight, this was another thing. She wasn't about to enquire about that. The most strikingly bizarre event of all this, however, was the woman in the wheelchair, lifting a quivering arm, notifying to her driver to pause for a moment by the window to her hospital room. The woman looked across and down a little, holding her gaze on her eyes. She said only one thing, 'Jamambu' and wept a solitary tear. She didn't know if the sorrow was self-pity or fear for her own life. It terrified her and comforted her all at once.

Other patients in the hospital, some directly opposite her room, had relatives bring foodstuffs in for them. They prepared and cooked hot meals there and then on the stone floor. Even producing little cookers. That was one thing you could say of these people, they knew how to look after their own. Maybe they had precious little choice in the matter?

She was aware of malaria, the usual diseases associated with developing countries, which still lack the essentials of a clean water system and sewage disposal, typhoid, diphtheria, cholera. What she truly believed had been eradicated though was leprosy. It was evident here and she remembered several people in the city affected by the same horrible illness. She had barely been able to look at these wretches. But in the hospital, well here, they were all in it together. The woman in the wheelchair had served to confirm a sense of togetherness in more things the longer she stayed there. When the doctors had to order her back to England, aside from saving her from whatever had taken a hold of her, this would pull her away from becoming someone at home with another country. Even though this country had been through the ravages of a civil war and was yet struggling now. Its turmoil, its unease, the unsteadiness, there was a fulcrum for her, a central pivot on which to find an equilibrium, a peace.

BELINDI II

Around the school generally she found an air of good humour. It was refreshing for her, especially in light of how serious this place could get. She found enormous solace in the meetings she had with one or two of the staff in particular. The headmaster's secretary was always eager to pass the time of day with her. Normally discussing western ways, and otherwise men. She thought she had a good friend in her. This was another girl who had ambition, dreams, like herself. She realised they both strived to aspire to bigger and better things. She didn't fully appreciate quite how deep the feelings ran, until she had returned to England. Once there, she received a letter requesting assistance in finding a husband, a home, money. She had thought to herself, perhaps, she ought to have expected this?

There was also the art teacher. She believed she could relate to him too. It wasn't until she was studying the subject at university that she wondered if he had been the trigger that had ignited the fuel of inspiration within her?

The situation reversed itself in a way when in later years she thought she recognised her old friend and mentor in Manchester, of all places. He had followed his own dream and, after a successful exhibition of his artwork, he had gained a scholarship at university in her own country. She was both in awe of his capabilities and equally surprised with herself that she had maybe misjudged his talent, overlooked his gift even.

For amusement the school would wheel out the large television from the house where she stayed. The boys would sit on the grass at the foot of a slight hillock. Someone would sprint off to the Brothers' residence for the generator in case the power failed. Then she would sit amongst them and watch some old James Bond film. She had seen it a dozen times before, but it gave her the opportunity for company, allowed her to socialise with her class and reminded her of things terribly English, for when she was home-sick. The boys seemed to find Bond hysterical. Typical of teenagers, there were the usual noises of encouragement and amusement during various scenes. Then if the power failed, a huge sigh would resound and reach a crescendo until it was reinstated with the hooked up generator.

It was during the course of one such late afternoon when the most hysterical thing occurred. The reaction could not have been any more spontaneous than if 007 himself had leapt out from the screen at his spellbound audience and the anecdote for her long after she had travelled home was farcical always.

What happened took place in the middle of a high-speed chase in the film. A number of cars were racing about, the engines being pushed to their limits. Just as the sound was reverberating out of the sound system, one of the boys, who sat on the ground transfixed to the box, let out a shrill cry and flapped his arms about. He seemed to be pawing at one ear, like a dog, and his fellow school friends were laughing incredulously at his antics. She looked across to her right, in the direction the fuss was coming from, taking her gaze back to the film with half a squint so as not to miss the action scenes. But several of the boys were now leaping up. She thought she could make out a sense of urgency, perhaps panic even. It seemed to have got dark extremely quickly to add to her bemusement. A few of the boys she knew quite well, were hurrying over to her and shouting something in Belindian. She desperately wanted to know what they wanted. Did they need her help? In an effort to comprehend the situation, she stood up to get a vantage point across the area. Then it hit home. Bees. Bees. That was what they were trying to tell her. A sky full of them, like some dirty great big storm cloud. It wasn't an evening sky turning rapidly to nightfall, they were bees swarming towards them overhead, and now, increasingly all about them. Once she had got her wits about her, she started to worry that they might be those African killer bees. With the television still playing her imagination started to get carried away and she began to remember several films where bees played the lead role. God help them.

The thoughts and images spinning about in her mind and sending her into a panic almost, must have been written across her face, because the next thing she was aware of was being virtually lifted by a group of the older, bigger boys to a place of apparent safety, whilst all the while, everyone about her appeared to be in fits of laughter. She couldn't be entirely sure if they were simply hysterical like herself. She had heard about these incidences of mass hysteria, possibly she was a victim of one such phenomena now? She tried glancing between a shoulder or two but it was so difficult to see anything much about the school grounds anyway as dusk was falling and there was precious little illumination aside from that of the screen.

At some point, minutes no doubt, though seemingly hours later, she started to pick up on a sense of relief. Many of the boys now and in increasing numbers were joking with each other and even taking up their places before the film again. Panic over, she thought. There were still a number of fits of giggles and the word 'jamambu' was being banded about with fingers pointing in her direction, a sniggering mouth half-hidden behind a partially closed hand.

She was surprised she hadn't been stung at all. Utterly astounded that apparently nor had anyone else. Killer bees, she wondered behind her embarrassment. At least in this half-light, her flushed cheeks could only emit a warmth instead of giving her humiliation away.

She truly enjoyed her free time with the boys. They had invited her over to what was referred to as "the school hall" at some point. When she arrived they had set the room up with tables and benches as though she had come for an interview. There definitely appeared to be a panel of judges or similar there, made up of these schoolboys. She felt suddenly rather nervous again, yet she knew she didn't need to be concerned, they had all made her feel extremely welcome.

As far as she was aware the school had some interest in drama and she remembered she had intimated a liking for the odd play, here and there. At her own school during her 'A' levels, she had helped produce and direct one or two versions of an Oscar Wilde classic or similar.

When she spotted a genuinely happy group before her she started to calm down and remember the faces with whom she had come to share so much during her brief time in Belindi. They explained to her that they had taken a vote and democratically, even unitedly, had chosen her as their new Drama Chair-woman. Not since her secondary school when for some reason, unbeknown to herself, the staff had picked her as the Head Girl, did she feel quite so proud. It was a large responsibility to be sure, but she rapidly put things into perspective. Glancing again around the happy crowd who were waiting eagerly for her to accept the post, she allowed herself to show her emotions and nodded once to them in agreement.

From then on she hardly let her feet touch the ground, nor anyone she chose to play a part in the drama club. She searched back to her experiences at her private school in England. There she was amazed to learn the school had its very own theatre, kitted out with everything a person could ask for. Here they had a bombed outbuilding, half dilapidated from wear and tear, bullet holes for the interior design and a large portion of the floor totally missing for who knows what reason. Lack of funds possibly? Still, she made the best of the situation she thought.

Somehow or other she unearthed a few copies of a play in English. She spent hours photocopying what she had in her possession on the unreliable and often defunct copier, stored under lock and key in the headmaster's office. She was amazed they had one at all.

A growing number of boys seemed to be taking an interest in the story that their young teacher was auditioning for parts for a school production and she had to be quite professional in her decision-making as to who should take which part. Some of the boys didn't take their involvement at all seriously, though they were not always the younger ones. In the end it was actually one of the youngest boys who got the lead and he took it on with both hands, heart and soul, through all the rehearsals and every performance to the final imaginary curtain call.

Besides the film club and the drama society, she liked the fact her home at the school was an open house for everyone about her. The boys simply wandered in and out with their smiles and jostling. They naturally seemed awkward and generally vied for her attention more often than not.

One day an electric organ arrived. It had a stand and all the usual gadgets so you could make it sound like a brass band or a string quartet. Of course it meant she needn't travel across to the Brothers' residence quite so often, to use the piano there. Here at least she could be in good company and that way avoid slipping into melancholia.

She was interested to discover some of the boys knew how to play a tune or two. It made her think of her grandmother who was able to play a tune by ear, having only heard it once before.

The music brought an air of fun about the place. She felt herself again, not so much succumbed by the desperation about her otherwise, with all the sickness and corruption. With these feelings she and the boys more than enjoyed each other's company. They were growing in their fondness not only for the things they shared in common but for the hope they held for a future together.

Sometimes she would play the music system near the open door and boys passing by the house would just stop right there, outside on the sandy path and begin dancing. She would smile back at them. Watching their young limbs moving so beautifully, so perfectly, she admired them enormously. They were marvellous. It made her desperate that she wasn't a Belindian. She was a Jamambu who could never be just like them, only mimic them. That would have to do then, she thought.

So it was that she chose to teach the boys some of the dances she had learnt at home and to a few of the teachers too. When they were all up at the school hall for the play rehearsals, she would take up a few minutes at the beginning and end to show them how she danced back in England. Everyone enjoyed themselves. Well they practically fell over themselves with laughter; they thought they looked so strange and funny. It helped relax everyone and again brought them closer to her and she to them.

It got so that when the time came for their performance of the play, the dances they had learnt along the way took up a large portion of the production time. There was a grand finale, a track she danced to with a boy a little older than her. She felt exhilarated. He was her ideal everything, even if she was a teacher to him. She ignored her nagging conscience and let the laughter and applause wrap around her in one delicious gleeful episode of her life in Belindi.

Occasionally she took the school pick-up the opposite way out onto the main road to another town, specifically to a nightclub there. This was when she and some of the other members of staff could really get to know each other.

The group was made up largely of the crowd she shared the house with. One of this group was the school games teacher. She had always thought he looked a little too thin to be any sort of an athlete, but her suspicions were put aside when a colleague informed her he had once played football for his country.

It transpired later that he was in fact recovering from typhoid. She didn't think he ought to be drinking alcohol, but she really hadn't known him long enough to play the concerned, nagging friend. Instead, she would dance at this nightclub watching him do his own thing in the mirrors that encircled them both. They would sit for a moment to have a drink. Nothing would be said. He seemed that way with her most of the time. Perhaps he felt more comfortable like that? She didn't mind. He was good company, as long as she was included somehow.

There was one night when she allowed herself total self-absorption of the dancing and the music. They were at the club and a song was playing she recognised from back home. Her arms and legs lifted her up and around, all over that floor. She passed in a flash in front of the mirrors, catching only a fraction of a face for a moment. She looked down at herself, lost in the sounds around her. The music, the beat, the bass, the hushed voices, breathing, whilst circling her were clouds of cigarette smoke, mostly all of the same popular brand, 'Horseman'. Oddly, she wasn't really able to identify her own features when she was moving about the room like that, but really and truly it took her for a fraction of a second to a place that made her face her true feelings, home, and that couldn't be a bad thing, could it?

The games teacher was called Samuel. She spent as much time with him as she was able, but it was clear from the start his mind was elsewhere. Possibly it was his illness? The weeks passed and thankfully, as he recovered he seemed more at ease with her, even quite funny at times with those he knew well. They grew closer but she admitted to herself, unreservedly, he would never tell her he felt as she did. Why, she was so sure, she could not understand but there was some recompense when she learnt of a young girl who lived with her parents in Mutabi.

The girl came to Samuel's room at the school on a number of occasions and she tried not to show any interest in them. Even taking herself off on walks along the main road for hours, to be as far away from them both. It was ridiculous she knew, because she could not run away from herself, her feelings for Samuel, her love for him.

He became ill again. A chest infection and by now she realised it was money he needed. Whilst she was plotting some way to help him, she learnt he had already been tricking the school into giving him funding for this and that, which he had fabricated. Although she detested his ability to behave in this way, she had to accept the inevitability of it all, he had to help himself, just as they all had to out there.

Between the school nurse and herself they treated him for months with the medicines he needed. She became closer to him, to the point where she was by his bedside nightly caring for him, tending his every need, his every wish. He wanted to take, always taking. She kept on giving, never leaving him until he told her she could or should leave. Samuel became weaker in body, but she was making him stronger in mind.

He demanded stories from her. He had to know about England. She used her imaginative ways to draw him a picture in his mind's eye of the wonderful and exciting thrills that were waiting in a country so much more fortunate than his own. He had to hear more. He made her tell him. Sometimes over and over, whilst the drugs slowly slithered throughout his wretched body.

He got thinner still. There was nothing he could eat without his body writhing with it, rejecting every mouthful he tried to consume. She by now had metamorphosized into his chambermaid, his storyteller, his hope perhaps. She felt strangled but she wanted him.

She knew his body as well as anyone who shared a love of someone so much could in their situation. She toileted him even. There were no barriers now, no embarrassment, no shame, only sickness and perhaps death.

At some point he had a visitor. The parents of the girl he had been seeing before came to the school. They were with him for hours, while she could only wait and worry. They emerged and left as quietly as they had arrived. They looked sombre and when Samuel asked for her to come to him later that same day, she understood the reason for their mood. He had simply one thing to ask her and then he was his silent self again. He asked her what was HIV?

Immediately, she caught her breath. She had come so close in her mind to wanting him to love her back, but how near to death had she wished herself? This was not merely a chest infection. She could not be expected to care for a human being so painfully ill, not by herself, she was really but a child anyway.

It was about the same time that she was admitted to hospital when she heard from one or two of the boys from the school, Samuel was being nursed by his family at his home in Mutabi. She tried to tell herself he was better off there and she too. Of the girl he had supposedly caught the virus from, she knew precious little but believed her to be a gentle soul and she felt sorry for her and guilty too.

In the end, she paid him one last visit, when she learnt he had taken a turn for the worse. She had been discharged and ordered back to England for the necessary medication they lacked in Belindi. Before her flight was due, she travelled with some boys to the hospital where Samuel lay.

Nothing could have shocked her more than the sight before her. Mosquito nets half hid the limp, wasted bodies beneath them and among them, she found Samuel. He was nothing. He muttered a few inaudible sounds and ushered her towards him with but an ounce of strength. But all she had left to tell him now was that she was leaving. She didn't mean to leave him, but she was going to have to return to her own home again. He looked utterly shattered. It was the end of him, she believed.

B U N G E E !

There was a place inland she had read about, off the back of a flyer at a back-packers she had stayed at for a night or two. It said it was run by a couple, one German and one half Danish, half English. Well, at least she ought to be able to make some leeway with the latter. Perchance to even have a decent conversation about things that didn't revolve around surfing, waves and the like for once. In fact what really made the hostel sound more inviting - not to say exciting - than all the rest, was the small matter of the couple keeping horses there and yes, guests were allowed to ride them. Absolutely fabulous!

It wasn't too bad a journey to get to the area where the hostel was supposed to be located. Having said that, the actual lodge house turned out to be sited behind some extraordinarily large evergreens that made it altogether invisible from the road that passed in front. Having investigated back and forth up the same stretch for a good forty-five minutes, as well as stopping at what turned out to be an old derelict farm cottage to ask for a bed for the night, she finally made it.

The house was fascinating. Clearly the couple had gone to enormous lengths to make both themselves and any guests, who were successful in discovering them, as happy and comfortable as possible. The first scene that met her was of the German, Peter, and the Dane, his girlfriend, Chantelle, seated around a smouldering fire in their garden. They were supping from bottles of cider, a local brand, from the look of the label, cold too gathering from the condensation between their fingers. With them was an older man, in similar rough outdoor clothing and worn-in walking or farm boots. They were joking and laughing, Peter giving the fire the occasional poke with a long stick unaware of her arrival. On the grass, lying between the couple, was a wonderfully good-looking dog, a German Shepherd, and on her approach he was the first to sense her. He lifted his strong head from off his paws, splayed out and crossed over in front of him and pricked up his ears. Then opened his big jaws to reveal the whitest of teeth and a loving smile, by way of a greeting.

In fact, as soon as they had all noticed her presence, there was no stopping them in their efforts to seem as hospitable as anyone she had met for a while. Before she knew it, they had shown her not only to her room, which was certainly more adequate and far superior to any she had paid for before, but the entire plot. This included the stream-fed pond, complete with pet ducks, and naturally the horses, that looked well cared for, fittingly.

Before she knew where she was it was almost dusk and Chantelle had planted a third, or fourth, cider in her hand. They watched the dying embers battle it out for their attention with the haze of a yellowed moon, criss-crossed with wisps of cloud, all of it mesmerising.

Ahead of them, out there at this farmstead, was a mountain. It dominated everything and everyone about it, but it wasn't eerie, far from it. So the following day it rather shocked her as she skinny-dipped in the pond when she noticed one entire side of the mountain appeared black, whilst the remainder was otherwise lush, green and flourishing, abundant with wild flowers, grasses and such. Suddenly the blackness that seemed to caress this side from almost the summit down the east, flanked by at least two-thirds its height, was ominous and foreboding. It was as though the mountain had two sides to it and this dark side was watching her, leering at her.

She decided to find out what had happened and learnt from Chantelle there had been a fire not so long ago that evidently had swept down that side.

"It was sad" she explained.

"No one died, I hope."

"No, no, no. No, it was just such a shame that so much wildlife suffered. There are so many incredibly rare flowers about here and we all thought it was just terrible."

"Was it a natural fire? No one's fault I hope."

"Natural, yes. In actual fact, what is so amazing is how much re-growth there has been up there."

"You have an incredible place here."

"Thanks."

"Have you put it altogether yourselves?"

"Yes. It's taken us a while, but we're pleased with the result." She looked over towards the horses grazing in their paddock.

"Do you ride?"

"Yes. Well, I get by," she added hastily, not knowing what level of competence was expected of her.

"Come on then, let's go and tell Peter we're off for a hack into the woods for the afternoon."

"Great! You can show me around your beautiful countryside."

Whilst she was taking another swig of coffee, in an effort to get her wits about her somewhat more, her newfound friend, Chantelle, emerged. She had tacked up two of the horses and was bringing them around to the front of the house.

"Which one do you want?" she asked good-naturedly.

"The smaller one will suit me fine," she answered. Though when she had got up and into the saddle things didn't seem as she had expected. She had chosen this horse because, as usual, she felt she could physically control it, since it was almost small enough to be classed as a pony. But she had forgotten you should never under-estimate animals and this one, as short as it was wide, had something about it that unnerved her. Spirited horses she had come to respect. This one she just didn't trust. There was no way she was going to expect herself to come back from the ride with Chantelle unscathed.

"Actually, do you mind if we swap?" she asked Chantelle.

"Not at all ... there you go. Okay?"

"Yes, definitely."

"Ready?"

"Yep."

"We'll go up this track into the wood there first. Do you see?"

"Yes."

"Then if you stay close to me I'll take you up a pass to the top of that hill there. You'll get a wonderful view of the land from up there."

"Okay."

"All right. Let's go."

They rode away from Peter and the house at a walk that broke into a slow trot. Then as they reached the trees and the air about them began to feel cooler, Chantelle got her horse to speed up the trot, then kicked it on to get it to canter. There was nothing for it but to follow. For what seemed an hour at least she held on with everything in her, to prevent herself from either falling off or being beaten off by the hundreds of branches that seemed to hang down in front of her face. Some of the thinnest branches, which could probably be classed as twigs if she was honest, she just didn't see in time. Really and truly she needed to wear glasses but without her contact lenses, which she had already used up, she knew it was pointless to expect the glasses to stay on her face. Consequently, her face had been scratched by the trees they were flying past, and she feared for her sight.

Finally, her heart well and truly in her mouth, she watched as Chantelle emerged out and back into the brilliant sunshine. Slowing her own horse down and back into a gentle trot again she took the opportunity to calm herself and take in the view, avoiding Chantelle's gaze so that she wouldn't wise up to her anxious state.

"Wow! It's beautiful here," she managed to say between gulps of breath.

"Oh, this is nothing. Wait until we get up there," Chantelle declared, as she pointed up the narrow, crumbling, track ahead.

"Come on. It's worth the effort, I promise."

They got their horses to inch their way over the stony path, one leg in front of the other and eventually they made it to the top. Turning the horses around to face the outlook she found herself at a loss for words at the sight before her.

"You were right. It's stunning. It's like you're looking to the edge of the world," she told Chantelle.

"I've always thought so. I come up here when Peter and I have had a row. I guess it puts things in perspective. It puts just about everything into perspective. Do you agree?"

"I do. Yes. I don't think I want to leave this place."

"Ha, ha! You'll have to at some point, I'm sorry to say. It's our home."

It was those last few words that made her suddenly feel very sad and with the mixed feelings she had already she almost felt a little giddy.

"Are you all right? You look a little pale."

"Yes, I'm fine. Just homesick probably."

"Here. You should drink some water. Here, and let me help you with those scratches," Chantelle added, pouring a little of the water onto a neck scarf and dabbing at the pink, prominent lines on her cheeks.

"Thanks."

"We probably ought to be getting back. I should help Peter with the chores."

"Oh yes, all right. Ready when you are."

Chantelle must have sensed she was sounding in a hurry because suddenly she was dismounting and tethering up her horse.

"Come on. We've still got a bit of time yet. Peter can cope. Sit down for a minute."

"Thanks."

They sat quietly for a while, close to the edge of the hilltop, and shared the water between them before making their way back to the hostel.

Peter came out of the house with a chilled cider for them both. Then when they had got down wearily from the ride, he generously walked the horses about to the paddock and hosed them both down before releasing them back with their friends.

"So, how was it?" he asked.

"Exhilarating and calming at the same time, if that's possible. Exactly what I needed. It's always a good thing to come back in one piece after a ride too, I always think," she answered him.

"Well it helps, I always think," Peter teased.

"So, what are you up for next then?"

"I don't know. What else is there around here for a girl like me?"

"Let me think. You could always have a go at bungee jumping if you like a thrill."

"Seriously? Where can I do that?"

"Just up the road from here. You must have come that way. You know the bridge you came over?"

"Yes."

"There is a bunch of guys who have a bungee under the bridge. You bungee off and down to the river below."

"Do you know how expensive it is?"

"Depends on what you mean by expensive. It's meant to be a whole lot of fun I know that much."

"Why, have you done it yourself?"

"What do you think?" he grinned.

"And is it safe?"

"Safer than riding, most likely."

"Well, that's not difficult. I think I'd like to give it a go."

"Go for it! They're not usually busy this time of year. You might be lucky if you wanted to try it out tomorrow."

"Tomorrow?"

"Well, why not?"

"All right. But for now I think I could do with a shower, excuse me."

"Sure. There's plenty of hot water. You should find some clean towels in there if Chantelle has been doing her job properly," he said laughing.

"Thanks. I won't take long."

"Take as long as you like. We've got our own."

"Fine."

It was perfect. Hot and powerful, not unlike the horse she had felt under her only moments before. She emerged from a shroud of steam, a freshly laundered towel held around her and pattered over the wooden floor to her room to dress. The evening passed uneventfully, making conversation with her hosts and trying to calm her nerves before the attempt at the bungee the next day.

Surprisingly, she felt she had slept well. She said her goodbyes and expressed her gratitude for their tremendously warm hospitality. Then made her way back down the road to the bridge Peter had told her about.

On the face of it, she never would have guessed people were able to bungee from here. As far as she or anyone could make out, it was just a concrete bridge on the highway. It wasn't until you stopped and peered right over the side that you would be able to see the banner suspended there, advertising the world's highest bungee jump. Well, if she was going to try something a bit hairy, she may as well do it in style. She could see one or two punters milling around down below and then out of the corner of her eye, she caught a glimpse of someone jumping. The faint call of encouragement in the form of the catchphrase 'Bungee!' could be heard from under the bridge and seemed to be directed at the jumper. She watched with sheer horror as the person before her, suspended upside down, his legs held together at the ankles, sprang straight back up again, almost to the level of the bridge where he had leapt.

It was frightening the way her mind had gone quite blank. From the moment she made the decision to get down there and go through the necessary preliminaries, health checks and so forth, to beginning her short journey across the undercarriage of the bridge, all was a blur.

She knew she was afraid of heights, terrified really. So why was she putting herself through this? It didn't feel too late, even as she was gingerly making her way across with one of the organisers to the station from where she was meant to leap. But then, with every minute step closer she started to feel as though this was her destiny. The pull became ever stronger as she edged from the walkway and onto the main platform.

There was a music system blaring out some loud and exciting-sounding tune. The blood starting pumping faster now. Two of the men approached her with a whole heap of gear and proceeded to walk her to a bench where she was asked to sit down. There they busied themselves with strappings and buckles about her ankles. Above the music, one of the men called out the safety issues, most of which were focused on just how safe it was to bungee anyway. They were all positive and encouraging, constantly smiling throughout and boosting her confidence no end. She was smiling back at them, though through gritted teeth and trying with all her might not to shake with the trepidation she was feeling. She sensed she was in a quandary, there was no one there she knew whom she would be letting down if she bottled out, but she was so close now. She could just do it, just jump, bungee and that would be the end of it.

They were done with the straps. Her legs were bound tight by the ankles and two men taking her from under each arm assisting her in hopping degradingly to the edge.

"Look out, not down. Arms out from your side and on the count of five bungee. Ready?"

They didn't allow time for an answer.

"Five, four, three, two, one ... bungee!!"

The others had all joined in with the countdown, screaming out the word 'bungee' over the volume of the music behind them. Their cries melted away as the abyss opened up its gaping mouth in front of her. She was soaring. It was unbelievable. Then totally terrifying at the same time, to the extent she felt compelled to shut her eyes. This in turn super-tuned her hearing to the rush of the air as she shot downwards towards the river. Inside she was fighting the terror she was experiencing, willing herself to open her eyes again, but she couldn't and just at the moment she awoke to the thought that she had stopped, the bungee plucked her back up, dropping her as quickly again and again until it finally seemed to stop. It was over.

No it wasn't. As she hung there upside down, suspended by the bungee, springing ever so slightly and swaying gently in the breeze, she realised. It dawned on her that the webbing that bound her ankles might slide off the ends of her feet. Really concentrating on keeping as still as possible in the circumstances, she started to feel very concerned. How could those straps possibly stay in place when her feet were pointing straight? It didn't make sense. Gravity would take effect. Before she knew it she would be plummeting through the air for the last twenty feet or whatever it was, cracking her skull open on the hidden rocks below the surface of the river beneath her. That much was certain. A sense of survival took a hold of her and thinking desperately now, how she could help herself, save herself even, all there was she could do was to turn her feet up ninety degrees in an effort to keep the straps on and save her own life.

She remembered there was supposed to be a member of the crew being winched down to bring her up again. Where was he? Come on, come on! She thought to herself. Panic was setting in.

"Come on, come on, hurry up" she found herself saying out loud now, then as she turned her attention back to keeping her feet in 'salvation' position there came a faint sound. It seemed to be a squeaking noise, getting a little louder now, though the sound seemed to come and go, almost rhythmically. What was it? It was like something or someone was trying to distract her from her feet.

"Well done! Fantastic bungee, Sarah!" It was the winch and on it one of the men who had persuaded her that throwing herself off a bridge well over two hundred feet above a roaring river was a sound idea. The fear still hadn't quite left her as she gladly wrapped herself around her saviour. With relief she felt the two of them being tugged in slow, jerky movements back up towards the awaiting smiling faces of the remainder of the crew. The winch just couldn't move fast enough for her.

At the top she still had to negotiate clambering off the man and the winch and back across onto the platform. The sound of the music system came to her ears again, amidst the applause, whooping and general congratulations all round.

"I bet you didn't think I would do it," she said to them.

"Well done! Really well done!"

T A M A U R I

She returned to England for a while. Recovered and recuperated from the malaria, she proved the doctors wrong and stuck it out at university. But now she was about to embark on more exciting and adventurous times. She was going to the other side of the world in every way and eager to get started in her new role as a polo groom.

On the way she had met some unusual people. Stopping in Thailand, the Philippines, where somehow she found herself at a business function held at the Ambassador's residence, then on to Australia. Now she was focused. For the next six months or more she was going to be living on a sheep farm in a place called Tamauri.

The family she was with would be expecting her to help out where she was needed, whether she had experience or not. Still, she believed she was prepared to get her hands dirty and that was precisely what she did!

The sheep farm was enormous. There was no doubt in her mind. This was the most impressive piece of farmland she had seen or imagined and what amazed her most was that the men who jointly owned the place knew every inch and each one of their stock.

They had help, in the form of dogs. They were sheep dogs, but not as she knew them. These were a mixture of sheep dogs, some were bred for their ability to run fast, some to bark the sheep into order or submission, others to simply look at the sheep to gain their respect and get them to do as they wished. They were known as 'eye-dogs'. Besides the dogs, the men had local friends who helped each other in a land of co-operatives. Sometimes they lent each other farm machinery, or manual labour, giving up their precious little spare time when things were busy or busier than usual. There was an untold number of tractors and farm machinery paraphernalia. Some of it didn't look as though it could be of much use but these people could turn their hand to most things and would do their own mechanics where it was required. Anything to save time or especially money when the farm sucked up so much of the stuff by the hour, literally.

She soon began to understand quite how much there was to do for everyone. Life on a farm was not easy and they were not about to make her feel as though she had come to holiday either. For seven days a week there was something that needed fixing, mending, harvesting, ploughing, depending on the season naturally, but the stock, the sheep, they were an ongoing concern.

At least with the sheep she could feel she could be of some help. Since she had no idea how to drive any of the farm machinery, she could at least exercise the polo ponies and check that the sheep hadn't got themselves into any trouble in the process. This side of her working life out in Tamauri she thought was fantastic. She was a free spirit, her own boss. This was most certainly the life. The life she had predicted or, at the very least, hoped for when she had first heard of the position back in England.

Each day, early in the morning, she would rise with the family she was lodging with. The only person not present at the breakfast table would be Scott, the father. He would have been about the farm, by horseback, checking his land for this and that and catching up with Ben, his brother and partner in the farm business. They would share a joke and somehow decide what needed to be done that day. It was all about prioritising. If half the chores were partially finished, they had had a result. She quickly understood the way of things and it made her reassess her opinions of farming back home. Even though it might appear as though a farmer had left his equipment and machinery lying idle, she could now appreciate it was more likely it had been parked up out of harm's way, awaiting a spare part to be borrowed from another farmer, who had been tied up with a dozen other pressing tasks.

When they weren't working, they were, it seemed. If Scott planned on joining his sons at a polo match at the weekend, it meant he would have to work double fast and twice as many hours, if that were possible. In a sense, there was no such thing as a free holiday. The farmers would help each other out, but really it was your lot, your responsibility, though their pride wouldn't let it show it bothered them. Sometime later, she learnt a statistic that confirmed her disbelief as to how these guys held it together. Their country had the highest suicide rate, globally, as far as farming is concerned anyway.

As for herself, her days weren't as long, but during her time out there, living on the farm, her weeks were arduous. If she got to the ponies early enough she could set to and have a few of them exercised by midday. Then as the warmer, hotter months approached, the afternoons riding the rest of the team would prove a hard task. This was certainly something she hadn't anticipated. She had always imagined if she ever had the opportunity to work with horses or ponies, she would never, ever, tire of riding them. But she quickly started to wish she had someone to hand the reins over to, when the pressure was on. This was understandably the case during and around the polo season, in particular. Then it really felt to her as though everyone else knew exactly what they had to do and how to do it, no matter what pony they had, green or otherwise, how complicated the tack required or how hard a taskmaster they had for a boss. She, on the other hand, knew only what little she had picked up from a few voluntary evenings spent after work at a polo yard back in England, prior to her trip out here and now, just as she normally did, she was otherwise winging it.

Whilst she was left to her own devices with the ponies, that was all well and good. She came to learn aspects of the job, sometimes where she had been shown how to do something, such as tie a certain knot, by repeating the process. Initially, there seemed a lot to remember, but she picked up a fair bit, just by having to do the same tasks six or seven days a week. Other times, she felt rather proud of her self-taught approach, which translated, in all honesty, was more like learning by her own mistakes, and at times, those were painful mistakes.

She remembered a time she felt very clever with herself, for teaching or re-training a pretty little grey to stop by the sound she made in her ear to her and change direction. The pony was as quick as lightening and as swift to halt and change direction if she had a care to. From her own perspective she and this grey made the perfect partnership. Maybe her boss would be so delighted with her talent at training this pony to respond like this he might even give the animal to her to keep? Well, she deserved it! Instead though she was given an earful. She soon came to understand how it was out here in Tamauri and probably most places like it. The animals, though sometimes apparently kept as pets, were generally 'speaking' toys or tools to be used when their users wanted them for their purposes.

Her boss sort of explained that if he had wanted or needed the pony in question to decide the way of the game, he might have asked her to try some trick she had thought up or had up her sleeve like that. But he had to know he could depend on this express train of a four-legged beast to stop and start and turn where the player saw fit. She didn't give up with the ponies, only some of the people the animals seemed to be forced to work with. She worked out that the ponies all had capabilities and personalities unique to them. One might only get fit if it was lunged for hours on end, rather than let her ride it. Another, eventually allowed her to mount him, but then would only ride in one direction! She noticed this was always towards the house and couldn't understand why, until one morning when Scott was about and he gave the pony half of his breakfast, which in this case was a piece of toast and homemade Tamaurian marmalade.

Scott was a true gentleman when it came to the ponies and an artist when it came to the troublemakers, ponies and men alike. He just had a way of dealing with situations. He seemed to be the only one about the place with any heart. His own pony he rode all about the farm and would hose him down when he was ready for a drink of something himself. Theirs was a true partnership.

He taught her to drive his old tractor once, at least that was the idea. When she clearly wasn't getting the knack of it, he just laughed it off. He didn't get annoyed or ridicule her. There was no sense of shame in any of it. With the ponies too, he was the first to volunteer and take her out across a part of that vast farm he owned with his own pony and show her the way of things for them. He put her at ease when she knew all too well, all eyes were on her to show them what she knew, to prove she was as good as her word. She had travelled around the world on the back of a promise she would be given the opportunity to work with these polo ponies and she was going to prove to them she was competent in the saddle, if lacking in confidence.

The confidence grew though. It took a knock here and there, along with her pride and she had to put up with the aches, pains and criticisms from the ponies and the boss. After a while though, she really began to believe in herself and that was what it was all about, not only the position she held here on the farm in Tamauri, but for herself, since she had tried to persuade herself that she was going to be alright again when she left Belindi and Samuel.

A typical day for her, on the farm with the ponies, would start with a walk down the long drive from the house. As it turned into the yard, where the tack room and hay barn stood, she could see one or two of the ponies out amongst some trees to the right. Then it was a case of taking out a handful of halters to catch the animals and bring them into the yard to tether up and give them each a good grooming. Most of the time this was more easily said than done. She learnt how to out manoeuvre them, how to outwit them, even. Well, there was definitely no way she was ever going to be able to out run them, that was for sure.

After a while, the ponies came to know her too. One of them, in particular, the grey, would wait until she was up so close, then twitch her ears backwards, having her back to her, and bolt off in any direction she chose, but clearly the opposite one. Another pony, the cleverest she felt, would lie in a hollow in the ground, where the soil was virtually like sand and therefore, softer and drier than the rest of the shady glen. Then as she came nearer, desperately trying not to let the metal hoops of the halter clank together, as she grasped them in anticipation of the catch, behind her back, out of sight of the pony, she would be up and out of that marvellous rest of hers and off. That pony, especially, seemed to have a hold on the others and kept her on her toes right to the end of her stay.

She was delighted when the time came and after not too long a wait either, that she was given the opportunity to ride this particular pony. Up until then she had only ridden the quietest of the team and apart from that had either led one or two of the others and lunged the difficult ones. Sometimes, she didn't feel she could be at fault for her lack of riding expertise, if a pony was green to her. That was to say, if the pony had been left out of the scene, more to the point she couldn't be expected to practically break the animal in, could she? This pony was neither. She had been around the block a few times and seen her fair share of polo tournaments into the bargain.

She worked out that ponies, or maybe it was only polo ponies, had a preference as to who they would work or play beside. When she took the chance to ride the leader of the pack, or the dominant mare, she was taking on a pony that commanded respect. The pony had an attitude. It had a sense of humour. She could be sure of herself one minute and totally out-done the next. But eventually both this pony and the grey worked best with her, if not for her. They still chose which direction and the speed they would travel at, across the many paddocks that made up the farm. She merely pretended that was her decision in the first place, went with them, in the hope if they were being watched, she was at least working them. At the same time and with the same method of madness, she clung on, attempting to appear as elegant as she clearly was not, in her riding stance. She rapidly ditched the English rose look, with the black velvet riding hat and jodhpurs, and adopted a baseball cap and shorts with farm worker style, clod-hopper boots, a nice brown shade to go with the mud or muck she often fell in.

Aside from riding and grooming the ponies, she had to ensure they appeared fit. She recalled the day her charming boss declared how utterly worthless she was as a groom, since she had missed the fact that one of the ponies, the one she had a tendency to ride the most, since she was the kindest of them all, had saddle sore. The truth was she hadn't noticed it, because she didn't know it was her responsibility to look for such things and wouldn't have known to look or what she was looking for anyway. Luckily, her boss was well vested in ailments horsey of this nature and he quickly took the sap of an aloe vera plant, which had been sat in the kitchen where she stayed all this time, applied this to the offending area, about where the pommel, or front of the saddle sits and hey presto in days, the old girl was as right as rain. Couldn't she have picked up such basic knowledge as to have prevented this happening in the first place? Perhaps she really was as incompetent as her boss was making out?

She remembered about this time something that happened to her at a job interview in England. She was asked a question, gave the first answer that came into her head and the next thing she knew, she was not only being offered the position she was applying for, but a promotion into the offing, supposedly promised before her trial period would be due to finish. Nothing came of the worthless empty promise, though she stuck at the initial job for a while. What she lost in wages, by missing out on the promotion, she gained in her understanding that she was someone who had her moments. Hers was a hit and miss kind of mind. She remembered her school reports to be a lot like that, reading that she could at times surprise everyone by her erratic spurts of brilliance. The thing she knew you had to achieve more than anything, because you could apply it to every worthwhile job, person and in many situations, was to get the person concerned to like you, first and foremost. In the case of her boss, she later realised she had tried too hard and only succeeded in him not simply ostracising her but nearly having her dismissed and deported back home.

If she wasn't going to woo him and charm the pants off him with her female wiles, then she would do everything in her power to be seen to be a good worker and gain his respect that way. So, she toiled away in that tack room, when she wasn't perspiring in the saddle, on the backs of those ponies of his. There was tack to clean, boots to polish, kit to have looking spick and span, ready for the next practice, game or tournament.

There was a radio in the tack room and when she worked in there, she would have it on for company. She hadn't really imagined she would be the only one down at the yard when she initially accepted the post. Although she never got used to the idea of working alone, the music and small talk from the radio station, based wherever it was based, was a help. Then there was always the daily few minutes with Scott and Ben. Talking about the way of things as old men sometimes like to. The old days. How the farm had taken shape. Sometimes they discussed how she was working the ponies and generally all seemed okay to her, from their viewpoint anyhow. When the sons were mentioned, though, which included her boss, that was another matter. She was being accepted by these elderly gentlemen. They were trusting her with personal information, with their own opinions as to how they felt their boys were behaving, with all and sundry. The way they worked this farm and others, which she learned belonged to the family too. Their relationships between themselves, with people she had met around the polo scene. Situations involving marriages being on the rocks, which she had been under the illusion, until then, that they were as safe as houses. They were opening up their world to her, as complex as it was conformist. This was their own personal dynasty, with all its travesties. She might not be all that much good at her job, but she had got them to like her, at least those that mattered most, the good eggs amongst them.

Outside of the tack room she would find an inner world about her, comprising the farm dogs, other work going on and family life, though not hers. One of the farm dogs was allowed to behave like a pet. He wasn't tied up by a chain to his kennel, like the working dogs. He was patted and accepted into the house, even given tit-bits, from time to time. He was a little dog, a terrier type, she thought. Very friendly, which certainly helped to get her through the working day, otherwise alone, but for the radio. When she was out with the ponies, she would have to tell the dog to stay behind, which he duly did, mostly around the tack room and the hay barn, which seemed to be his favourite spot anyway. No doubt, this was owing to the numerous rats he could find and chase about the place. If she didn't order him to wait for her return, he would be irritating the ponies, by yapping about their heels. Riding was a dangerous sport, in any case, without this extra trouble. She knew well enough, she shouldn't be riding without a hat, but it added to the thrill and she was still very young and invincible.

Aside from this dog, the family owned a cat and again, it was kept more as a pet. Apart from when one of the men came in from work, hot under the collar in more ways than one and the cat would double up as a rugby ball and be kicked from behind, across the room it had happened to enter, to its misfortune.

When she hadn't been on the farm very long she decided to make her mark and tidy the tack room. After all, this was going to be her main place of work and she had never been able to work in a mess. She thought she made a good job of it and for once she managed to please her boss and even achieved a smile out of him. Word got about and at this point she realised she was definitely in his favour. This was confirmed when he told her he needed her to come and stay on his own farmstead, down in Wamawatungi. A beautiful place, which if you stood at its highest point, you could glimpse the sea to one side and the mountains to the other. They told her you could find whales at the coast there and she would strain her eyes at times to try to make their shape out on the dazzling crests of the ocean.

So it was that when there wasn't too much work to do with the horses she would stay down with her boss at his farm in Wamawatungi. There they were like a husband and wife team.

He got on with the heavy farm work. She got stuck in where she could and when he allowed her. The only pet was a lonely bull, kept in its own paddock, with its own glimpses of the heifers, lying across to its right, nearest the sea. Bizarrely she became quite relaxed around the bull. Ever since she had paid good money to watch a bullfight, somewhere on the Spanish coast with a girlfriend, she had felt some sort of empathy for this creature. The bull then was strong and forceful, with an amazing willpower, but would be jabbed at and poked until all its strength had gone. What had it done to deserve that? Nothing as far as she could make out. She somehow managed to make a correlation in her mind of how life can be sometimes. Try as you might, in every way you know how, some people will take sport in pushing you around.

For her, there was the housework, the gardens, and meals to attend to. Not an ounce of riding or grooming to be done. But, really she didn't mind all that much. She could have a break from the horses and here she had some company for a large portion of the day.

This was fun. She enjoyed playing housewife, especially for her boss. It seemed to please him, perhaps to soften him a little? She felt as though she was becoming more like the people around her, working hard and therefore enjoying the breaks and the play times even more so, because they were so well deserved and so badly needed.

When he came in from his day's work, she would be there for him with a good, hearty meal, always something she knew would please him. The house scrubbed. Some other section of it looking as tidy as she could make it, without throwing away any of his things. She didn't want to be seen to be taking over. She was still his employee and a visitor to his country, a guest per chance. The gardens looked relatively tidy too, considering it would only take a blast off the coast inward to blow all the dry leaves, scrub and debris, back. Over the little, winding footpaths she had spent all morning sweeping, in spite of the blisters.

There came a point when there felt as if they had a sort of connection between them. When he finished for the day and they had eaten together, they would sit, watching some old film or other and he would accept her a little and even allow her to sit beside him, close on the sofa. They talked a little, but there was always that void between them that comprised her lack of knowledge of farm work and the intensity of it all and his inability to accept their differences as anything more than a nuisance.

Not put off, she concentrated her efforts on the better side of his personality and the relationship she thought was growing between them. One night she could bear it no longer. She crept from her bed and across the hall to his room. Since the house, just like many in the area, was only a single storey, at least she didn't have to face any creaking stairs. Then, suddenly, she was lying beside him. Lying in that wonderful warmth he was generating. That smell of his was all around her, all encompassing. Dare she touch him? She longed to, but would he mind? Would he lose the plot completely and throw her out on her ear there and then? She tried to calm herself, so that her breathing wouldn't wake him. What a night! Even if he never stirred, she was lying there with him, that in itself was almost enough. Then, quickly, silently he spun around and grabbed her. She held her breath. The night sky shone its light about the room and across one side of his head, like a lighthouse, as the clouds scuttled across the face of the crescent moon. She couldn't tell if he had the look of a man about to kill her, or embrace her. She held her breath for what seemed an eternity and like a snake, he struck. He was stronger than she imagined and she pictured the bull, tethered to the old cedar tree below the window, and shivered. He had her shoulders in the palms of his hands, his fingers, dirty and warm clasped over her back, holding her tight and then he pulled her to him. In one movement he lifted her up to his chest, then as easily spun her on to her back and was on top of her. Striding her like some mighty Colossus. She knew then that he wanted her too. They moved their bodies together, so close and breathing rapidly now, their hearts almost erupting out of their chests and colliding into each other. Then, as suddenly as it had all begun, he chose to stop. He took control and she slipped away as silently as those clouds outside. Moving only like a shadow she made her way across the darkened room to her own again. In a moment she could hear him snoring and she was alone once more with her thoughts, her anguish, her passion.

By the morning it was clear he had regretted the previous night, though it had amounted to virtually nothing. He told her it wasn't working having her there and she would have to return to his parents' farm and stay at their house in Tamauri.

She returned almost straight away, and feeling silly, childish even. Knowing all about her, probably they were aware of what had gone on between them. She had practically thrown herself at him and he had rejected her. When would she learn to have more dignity and self-respect? But life is complicated as much as humans can be and she wasn't aware of all the facts at that stage.

EN ROUTE
THE MAN WITH THE TATTOOS

It was when she was winding her merry way to Tamauri that she happened to come by a hostel that offered complimentary breakfasts and, more essentially, it had vacancies. She felt confident in her find initially, almost pleased with herself that she had managed to bag somewhere on her tight budget, that had a pool.

It had been difficult trying not to spend anything much at all when she was travelling through so many wonderfully beautiful countries en route. She saw clothes, jewellery, paintings, ornaments that attracted her, tempted her. The designer rip-offs were just too much for her to resist though and she treated herself to a Gucci handbag and several Ralph Lauren polo shirts in Bangkok.

Having found a bunk bed for herself and even a spare one for her backpack, below, she pulled out a bikini top, swapped her blouse and made her way to the poolside. Amazingly, no one else was there at the time to share it with her. What utter luxury. She bent a little, sideways on, and dipped a toe in the water. It felt a bit chilly, but she thought she could get used to it. Crouching down to sit at the side, she dangled her feet in the blue crisp water. Pure indulgence. It pleased her to think how hard she had needed to work to save the money for her ticket. How now already it all seemed worthwhile.

The sun was doing its worst, beating its relentless rays onto her near naked back. She looked about her, got up again and pulled off her shorts, revealing the matching bikini bottoms beneath. Adjusting the elastic in that unattractive way women do, she walked over to a metal ladder that leant its way into the pool. The temperature was still a shock to her, but only for a moment. Holding her nose she submerged herself fully into the depths, coming up and wiping the wetness from her face before opening her eyes again.

There he stood. A man twice her build and age by the looks of him. Tanned all over with leathery patches that gave away his worshipful ways to the sun. She didn't imagine he would bother with protection, but she hesitated to assume anything of him at that point, except he didn't seem too bothered about self-harm when it came to tattoos. It was very evident his shoulders were covered in them and as he bent forward to dive into the pool she saw how the motto continued down his back. He reached the opposite end and turned to swim back again. There she could see the artwork in all its glory. It was the image of a serpent. Its head was snaking its way about the waist of a naked woman, with hair that cascaded down in front of each breast. About her feet was a long chain that seemed to almost merge with the pattern on the skin of the monster that threatened her. There was some writing that she didn't recognise as any language she had read before. Maori maybe? She wondered what it translated as and marvelled at the scene.

He reached the end, placed his palms on the side, then hoisted himself up and around. The swiftness of his movements was almost a shock for her. Was that the extent of his exercise routine? She wondered how else he built up those enormous muscles and kept himself so trim? Her eyes flicked up and down his rippling abdominals. She counted them. Six, perfect. As for that chest, a sprinkling of hairs, more to the right than the left, and pectorals any man or woman would die for.

She jumped, realising the man she was ogling had noticed the attention she was giving him.

"All right?"

"Yes, fine thanks. How are you?"

"Good, yeah. You're English, right?"

"Right. And you're ... Australian?"

"Maori."

"Oh, okay."

"But yes, Australian."

"Do you work near here?"

"Yeah."

"Right ... what do you do?"

"This and that, mostly this."

"And what would 'this' be?"

"You ask lots of questions don't you?"

"I guess so. Sorry."

"That's okay. What's your name anyway?"

She wasn't sure she wanted to tell him. There was something not right, something about him that unnerved her, muscles or no muscles. She lied.

"Amanda."

"Good day, Amanda. Pleasure to make your acquaintance."

"And yours?"

"Jerry. My cousin owns this place" he explained his presence.

"Jerry ... are you staying here?"

"No. I'm at my brother's. He's looking out for me, putting work my way, you know. It's been a bit difficult lately."

"I'm sorry."

"That's all right. It wasn't your fault. I've just got out of prison."

"Oh, prison?"

She was really shocked now, almost afraid. Should she pry even more into his private life, his deep, dark sinister past? Maybe it was something and nothing.

"Can I ask what for?"

"I killed my sister's husband," he claimed matter-of-factly.

Deathly silence for what seemed an eternity. She found herself bouncing up and down in the water in an effort to shake off the goose bumps his comment had caused. Wiping an imaginary hair away from her face, she cleared her embarrassed throat, then waited an eternity for him to justify his actions. A murderer, a murderer? This couldn't be happening.

"He raped her. The police weren't doing anything. She was too frightened to go to Court. No one was doing anything. She's my kid sister. So I wiped that smirk from off his face for him."

She wondered how he did it? Wondered if it resembled some East End gangland assassination? She shivered.

"How long did you get?" she asked him, trying to take her mind off the thought of what he was capable of.

"Too long."

What did that mean? He should have been locked up for life. A life for a life. Then again, maybe there is such a thing as mitigating circumstances? After all she was raped by her husband. That was a crime in itself, wasn't it? Maybe he got his just deserves. But no, she didn't believe whatever their reasons, that anyone had the right to take a life. That surely was God's domain? She sensed inwardly she was getting on her soapbox again. Instead, she wondered how the wife felt, the sister to a murderer? Was she now scared of her brother in place of her husband? She felt confused, nervous. This was too much for her.

"What's with that tattoo?" she asked, trying to change the subject somewhat.

"Oh, that?" he answered, as though he had forgotten it was there. "It's simple. The woman you see there is my sister, Angela. The serpent is me."

"And the chain?"

"That mad bastard I got locked up for."

"Oh, I see ... what does the writing mean?"

"It's Maori for 'free the good spirits to roam with their kin again'."

"He was a bad spirit then, I guess?"

"Evil, pure evil. He will never rest. He has no home here or anywhere now."

"Does your sister have any children?"

"No, thank Christ, she can't."

"Oh, sorry."

He smiled at her slightly as though to say, why do you English always feel responsible for everything that's wrong with the world?

"What about you then? You staying here?"

"Yes. Well, for a couple of nights ... maybe." She wasn't too keen to stay in a hostel with a murderer for company. Perhaps she should book out now? No, that would be too obvious. He could take offence, possibly follow her, stalk her? God, when her back was turned he might be rifling through her things, steal her passport? She didn't know even if he had got a taste for it now? What if she was next, victim number two?

"Are you looking for work?" He interrupted her train of thought. Did he want her to work for him, and his brother, doing 'this and that'?

"No, I'm fine, thanks," she snapped nervously.

"Well, I wasn't about to offer you a job you know. Just making friendly conversation, being polite you know."

He made her feel guilty. She was judging him. He couldn't blame her, surely?

"Sorry, I didn't mean anything."

"No, you're all right."

Great, he liked her. Hopefully she wasn't on his 'A' list after all.

"No, I'm heading off to work as a polo groom in the next day or two," she informed him, omitting to tell him where she would be heading off to.

"Horses, yeah. They're great creatures, truly wild. Wonderful spirits. They're like men, you know, you can't tame them, not really. They'll work when they're in the mood, if they like you, if you're kind to them. But only as long as they want to. Don't fool yourself that you're in control of them, ever. They run with the wind because it is a free spirit like them. Watch them. Take the time to study them when they're not aware you are there. You'll see them dancing. They were born workers; they'll keep at it until they drop down dead with exhaustion. Their hearts are so big. Like the wind, though, when we're not trying to control them, harness them, they can be a force of their own no man can match. Angela understands them, she's great."

She wasn't too sure what to say after that speech. He was right of course, absolutely. It seemed incredible she had something in common with a killer. She thought she would go away remembering what he had said. Wise words.

"I'm going to go in now. It was nice meeting you. Thanks for the advice."

"No worries. Catch you later."

She felt her heart miss a beat, almost, but reminded herself of his beliefs in the spirit world and she was okay with that.

THE COAST, THE ANGEL AND
THE GERMAN

She discussed the place whilst talking with some Australian hunks who were running a back-packer's. They had it sussed, a colourful, alternative hostel of sorts, right smack on the beach. It was a beautiful stretch of coastline, not quite surfers' paradise, but close enough. But having explored the local talent over the course of the last few days she felt she had seen enough. It was testosterone town out here. She hooked up with a small group of English travellers, heading for a place inland slightly, known as Horses Hollow. The Aussie hunks had recommended it to her. It turned out many of the hostels had arrangements between themselves, both on a friendly and a business relationship. They each advertised one another's premises with fliers, posters and the like. She had been making specific enquiries as to where she could go riding. Only to learn less than an hour's journey from where she had been staying was a hostel run by another German guy who had connections with a nearby riding establishment. What was it about Germans and horses anway? If there were enough people in her group interested he could organise a hack for them. Thrilled at the prospect of getting back in the saddle and getting some practise in before she took up her position as a groom, she packed up her things and headed off with gusto.

They arrived late in the evening. Freddie, the German, was nowhere in sight. She was beginning to wonder if she was alone in worrying if they had taken the wrong route and had arrived some place else? Everyone began to pile off, so she guessed she ought to follow suit, grabbing her backpack by the straps and squeezing out, one sideways step at a time to the gangway. Peering out of one of the windows of the bus, she spotted a couple of longhaired, hunched-backed feet dragging, sandal wearing, dope smoking, twenty somethings. She caught a glimpse of their faces as they turned to acknowledge the arrival of the bus. Men, well just, but not bad looking, under all that facial hair and the attempt at dreadlocks. She had heard, allegedly, that some people didn't seem to feel the need to wash their hair once it was like that, for months! Her imagination began to run wild once again and she had visions of bugs, nits and all sorts crawling through their mangled mops. Well, who was she to talk? She could do with a good soak herself. Live and let live. She jumped down off the last step from the bus and followed her travel companions over the freshly mown lawns towards the house.

There was a dark hallway off the entrance, an attractive looking side table, mahogany perhaps, that stood before her with an ornate oval mirror above. The look was very homely. On top of the table had been placed a book, with a pen beside it, tied to a piece of string. She moved closer, glancing over several pages of previous visitors' names, addresses and comments, all very complimentary. One or two guests had come from England, Somerset and Glasgow. It was all so specific that it made her feel slightly homesick. Someone's voice from just behind her, coming into the house, made her turn.

"Welcome, welcome everyone. You are all most welcome. I trust you have all booked in and found somewhere to lay your weary heads. My name is Freddie; I will be your host for the duration of your stay here. You should know that this is my home, please use it as your own, relax and enjoy."

With that he then proceeded to repeat his welcoming speech in French, German, Spanish and what she thought might be Portuguese. The whole flourish came with the silent accompaniment of Freddie's doting German Shepherd. Was this a dream? Another German Shepherd to match the horse-loving Deutschman? It was touching how warm a double act they were together. They seemed to have got their roles down to an art, seemingly making everyone about her instantly more relaxed. Something she hadn't thought possible.

Freddie finished and some of the group were about to dispense to various areas of his home when he called them back unexpectedly.

"Sorry, sorry folks. A word or two more if you please. I only ask for you to refrain from smoking, whatever it is you care to smoke, in your rooms. This is for fire safety, yes?"

There were a few titters at the innuendo and a general understanding and agreement with regards to his extremely sensitive, polite and well rehearsed request.

She watched with interest as their host swept out to the porch, bent down to a pile of ready cut to size logs and brought in a basket load. Later, she heard the basket and a dozen or so others were woven by Freddie himself. It turned out basket weaving, wood chopping and speech making were only a few of his many talents. His skills also extended to cooking, brewing, of the alcoholic variety, naturally and transforming a grey, melancholy crew into a carefree enlightened band of merry men. This he was capable of achieving by a combination of the fantastically efficient log fires he built - pine cones an essential added ingredient - together with his wonderful guitar playing.

She sat beside two other travellers, squashed together on a tattered sofa that had seen better days, watching Freddie's movements. He was bent over, crouched on his tanned legs, the white of his heel visible on one foot which with lifting up from his shoe. He struck one singular match and the impressive monument before him was smouldering already. Not before too long the groupies in Freddie's home were sat about a beautifully smelling and enticing fire that crackled and hissed at them between the strains of Freddie's musical capabilities.

You couldn't help but admire and respect his capacity to keep the place running as a business, whilst at the same time appearing relaxed and ever cheerful. It was as though there existed another hour or two in his day. Somehow he was able to find opportunities to mix with his houseguests, even making an effort to get to know most of them, individually. The best thing about him was that he was genuine. He was likeable and therefore, understandably, his visitors returned again and again.

There was one person whom she had met only a short walk from Horses Hollow. A middle-aged, attractive English lady who ran a gift shop. It was such a remote area, she wondered if the woman earned enough to get her by? When she gave it more thought, it occurred to her there was this strong possibility the shop owner wasn't making enough to afford to get home to England again. Perhaps she chose to stay? She decided she preferred the latter idea as a guess at the woman's destiny.

Aside from the gift shop ex-pat, the surrounding area was essentially free of what could be termed the human race, as we know it. Replaced instead with foliage, an abundance of wildlife and a huge variety of the most striking fauna. It was enticing, captivating. To encourage the naturalist in her, Freddie sacrificed half an hour of his busy schedule to describe a walk she might enjoy.

"If you truly want to see this place for its real beauty you cannot - must not - leave before you have seen our Angel" he told her.

"Angel?"

"Follow the well-trodden path that leads straight out from the edge of the lawn there," he started, pointing out from the open doorway. "Keep on it, through the forest and down to the river. You'll find a waterfall there and if you look up you should see the Angel."

She wondered how long a walk he was talking, but hesitated to ask such a 'how long is a piece of string' question. Though Freddie was so easy-going she felt confident to ask him regardless.

"Do you reckon I'll be back before nightfall," she joked with him.

"Well, it's only after ten in the morning, so I would like to hope so" he said sarcastically.

"No, joking aside, what do you think?" She pondered as to just how long and how far she was prepared to walk for.

"Two, three hours tops."

That was all right. She could handle that.

"Fine, but if I'm not back for supper."

"We'll start the party without you, I know."

"Ha ha. Very funny. Bye, bye, bye."

To begin with the path she needed to follow was certainly well-trodden - almost to the point, whereby, she expected to see a section from a local ramblers society striding ahead of her, walking boots in motion in time to their individually carved sticks. Aside from that, all else that was missing were the obligatory public footpath, bridleway and other mandatory right of way signs. Then, as she went on, the path seemed to narrow. The tread under her foot was not too much the hospitable gentle sand as before, it was gravelly in places and now somewhat stony. Mentally, she cast her mind back to her school geography lessons and contemplated soil erosion. It helped take her mind off how uncomfortable her shoes were beginning to feel.

It wasn't too long before she made the decision to take off the offending items, then her top and fairly soon she was almost going commando style. Still, there weren't actually any ramblers about so why shouldn't she let go of some of that prim and proper English side to her for a change? The ground was still making her feet smart a little and now as the sun was starting to climb slowly higher into the cloudless sky, it was heating up the track she was following too.

She gasped. "A snake!" Catching her breath as a rather dull-looking, slightly mottled snake shot across the path in front of her. "Oh my God. A real, live snake" she said out loud in disbelief. Shocked by the idea that she should be in such close proximity to perhaps a lethal, creature she shuddered, then hurriedly looked all about her to learn of its whereabouts.

"Where have you gone, you slippery creature you" she asked aloud. The truth was that actually she knew full well snakes weren't slippery to the touch, contrary to popular belief. She had learnt that much at school after some visit from a travelling circus or more like the philanthropic ways of the local pet shop owner. It was nowhere to be seen. Relieved, for the time being, she carried on with her mission to behold the Angel of the falls, but the incident had made her awaken from her naïve stroll to an alertness that worst still bordered on the paranoid.

Up ahead, the way looked more lush. There were ferns fringing the now almost invisible track. Her bare shins brushed them aside effortlessly. She liked the way they felt cool against her skin. Mercifully the ground was more forgiving now too. In fact it almost felt damp.

As she walked on she thought she could hear the sound of running water. It instinctively made her bladder feel weak. Yet, at the same time, she realised just how thirsty she was. Looking up towards a canopy of deciduous trees she shielded her eyes from the glare of the brilliant sun and delighted in the silvery chains of what could only be the waterfall.

Now she had two incentives; her curiosity to meet this elusive Angel figure, and a raging thirst that she fantasised the river would satisfy. The spray from the fall was such that she could almost feel a fine down floating about her face and body teasing her senses. Bizarrely she felt she was almost able to smell the fall too.

All of a sudden the path became very slippery. Unable to keep herself upright any longer she slumped down on to her backside with a thud, her legs flying out in front of her.

"Oh, great. Fan-tastic," she scolded herself.

Heaving herself up again she repeated the action once again, cursing even louder.

"Having some problems there?" came a voice.

"Nope. I'm fine, thanks. Absolutely marvellous," she called back.

"If you had kept to the track I told you to you wouldn't be lying in a heap on the ground like that; your ass covered in mud," he rebuked.

"I did and, anyway, my ass is doing okay thank you very much. Mud is meant to be good for the skin," she retorted.

Whilst he was seemingly putting her down she had managed to grab hold of some plant life about her and using it she hauled herself upright. Keeping to one side of the track she started to tiptoe her way down the slope. Very quickly this method became too awkward as well and not wishing to make a fool of herself a third time, she chose to straddle the path instead. With her brown damp shorts and splayed legs she looked a sight, topped with the fact she was having to hold her arms folded over her bare breasts in case Freddie could see her. For sure, whatever his intentions she hadn't been able to spot him so far. What she had fathomed was that he had company, company in the form of a horse that was. She had clearly heard it snorting, clearing the dust, pollen and what have you from its nostrils.

"Anyhow, what are you doing all the way out here? Following me?" she asked him.

"Oh, a gentleman would never be so bold!" he teased.

"I wouldn't have mistaken you for a gentleman," she joked.

"Actually, I thought you were taking your time out here and knowing you English women ..."

"What are you getting at?"

"... and your lousy sense of direction, I guessed you could do with a guide. I guessed right by the looks of things. You seem to have mislaid a good number of items of clothing too, I see."

She gasped at the realisation she was visible, clasping her breasts even tighter, her fingers imbedding themselves into the flesh upon her ribs.

"Come out so I can see you too," she told him, arching her neck and twisting her head about her to catch a glimpse of him.

"Here I am," he said in a whisper. She jumped as he appeared behind her, sitting bare back on a striking looking horse. Its face black, save for a white star below its brow band. Its legs were half hidden in the undergrowth, but Freddie's were clearly visible, tanned, hairless and muscular.

"So I see!"

"I've brought one for you too. They're thirsty so if you can take this one off my hands for me, I would be most obliged," he asked of her, producing a chestnut mare on a lead rein from behind his own horse. Seeing the saddle on its back and the bridle, she felt relieved he wasn't expecting her to ride bareback too like him, particularly since she wasn't sure if she was capable.

She moved stealthily across to her mount and finding she wasn't as flexible as she had hoped, she unbuckled the stirrup leather and loosened it to bring the stirrup iron down to a more realistic level. Raising a leg she discovered she was still going to have some difficulties. The horse seemed to sense her anxious state of mind and began to prance about and scrape its front hoof on the ground impatiently.

"Steady, steady there girl" called Freddie.

She wasn't altogether too sure if he was referring to the horse or herself. Freddie by this stage had dismounted and leaving his ride to its own devices in complete mutual trust, he strode over to her aid. Lowering a hand to her foot he allowed her to use him, as he almost catapulted her up into the saddle.

"Okay? Are we set?" asked Freddie, effortlessly climbing up onto his own horse. Without a saddle he looked as if he had perfected a technique of throwing his chest over the horse's back then swinging his leg over behind. She marvelled at his agility.

"Follow me. It isn't safe for the horses if we carry on this way."

"Okay."

"Are you alright with jumps?"

"It's been a while. How high are we talking?"

"Don't fret. You'll be fine. These two know this area more than anyone. They're keen to get to that water too, and you can't blame them in this heat."

"Is anyone else joining us?"

"Not that I've been told but Emma and Jo could be bringing down a group early this evening for a twilight hack. Nothing confirmed as yet though. It's not worth their while if there isn't enough interest."

"Emma and Jo? I'm guessing they run the stables near your place?"

"That's the one. Are you happy on Nippy?"

"Oh, that's her name. Does that mean she's going to bite me when I'm not looking or she's liable to bolt?"

"Ha! Wait and see."

"Great. Thanks for the warning, I don't think."

The horses carefully clambered down to the riverbank, instantly lowering their necks down to reach the cool, thirst-quenching water. Their riders slipped off the side and cupping their hands they helped themselves to a long draught too.

"It's a bit late to ask, but since you're drinking the stuff I guess the water's safe?"

"Naturally. Nothing but the best for my guests. You might care to wear this, you look a little cold," he said, offering her the shirt that had been tied about his waist.

In her haste to reach down to drink she had neglected to cover her chest. Freddie hadn't been able to help himself. She raised her arms up into the sleeves of the soft garment and poking her head through she closed then opened her eyes in almost the same movement. There in front of them on the far side of the waterfall, refreshing himself in the river's delights was another man.

"Oh my God, he made me jump. I thought you said we were alone."

"No I didn't. What I said was as far as I knew. It just so happens I'd forgotten Father Sebastian occasionally comes down to delight in the greatly beneficial properties of the waters here, don't you Father?" he yelled the last few words over the noise of the river.

"What's that Freddie? Oh, got yourself a woman at long last have you? About time too! Looks more like a girl from here though. Aren't you going to bring her over and introduce us properly?" Father Sebastian called back.

"Sure, Father. Whatever you say." They left their horses at the bank and started to wade in, but as the depth of the water got to their waists and they could feel the gentle current twisting about their legs they both allowed themselves to float up and started to swim to the fall. It felt perfect; everything, the coolness of the river in that merciless heat, this young man by her side, seemingly looking out for her, yet not appearing to expect anything in return, at least not yet. It made a change.

When they reached Father Sebastian and the fall, the noise was quite deafening. She was astounded the men could make out what each other were saying, then she noticed something. Freddie was wearing a hearing aid and when she studied them she realised they were both lip-reading.

Freddie moved closer to the priest and placed his arms around him, his bare chest pressing into the other man's body. He laid his face sideways on to his black robe.

"Aren't you getting hot in these thick clothes?" Freddie asked, lifting his face to his friend to help him understand what it was he was asking.

"Black. I know, not terribly practical in this heat. I was about to, but you know how bashful I can get."

"Come, come Father. This lady is a friend of mine. She's well travelled like us. She's seen all sorts."

With that they kissed, not as friends but passionately like the lovers they were.

"Now come along, let's get this off you," Freddie told the priest. With that he teased off the long robes over Father Sebastian's head and into the water behind him, pushing the priest backwards to join them as he did so. There was a lot of tomfoolery, childish splashing and laughter. She felt uncomfortable and somewhat disappointed at the behaviour of the pair of them.

"What's the matter, young lady? Have you never in your life seen a priest cavorting with a man in a peaceful, natural place such as this before? Or do they all do it tucked away in closets where you come from? Don't panic yourself. We're not about to get down and you know what in front of you at least."

"No, I'm sorry. I've seen a lot of goings on that's for sure, but a priest - well, it's just I thought you said a vow or something."

"Oh that. Yes, celibacy. It's all right if you mean it. I'm as good as out of that monastery anyway. They won't move with the times you see and well, you can't help the people if you don't understand the world they live in, don't you think?"

"I suppose you've got a point. Where were you planning to move on to?"

"Well nothing is set in stone. Freddie's keen to be on his travels again so I might help a friend out and do some housesitting for him. Some of the people who come up here have no respect for nature you know and more to the point they appear to show precious little respect towards Freddie here either, isn't that so?"

"Well, I'm not sure you're entirely correct there, Father," Freddie told him with a smile.

"Of course I'm right."

"Won't they ... what do you call it? Dis-robe you or something?" she asked with concern.

"It looks like young Freddie here has made a good job of that already, hey. "Wouldn't you say, friend?"

"Well, you could lose the dog collar too," laughed Freddie.

"No, on the contrary. You may need that for when I get a bit frisky," chortled the priest, rolling his 'r' with the last word.

The men rolled about like schoolboys sharing a private joke and she began to feel like a gooseberry. Afraid she was lost, indeed. Freddie was merely fulfilling a promise, a romantic interlude with the faithless elder over there.

"Tell me, have you lost your faith entirely? I mean do you still believe in God and all that?"

"If by that you are alluding as to whether or not one can still advise about God, the Father, the Son and the Holy Ghost, whilst cherishing this truly magnificent and beautiful being he has placed on this planet, then the answer is 'yes, yes and yes again.' Can a man not have one heart and yet keep in it his love for all things? If not, then that is for Him and Him alone to judge. Purely my own humble opinion though you understand, don't you go boxing me up and slapping a label on me. I'm not one to care much for being stereotyped. Things are, how we say, slightly different out here. Some of us have broken free from the shackles man feels obliged to place on us."

"But I thought you entered a monastery of your own free will?"

"And so I did. But God doesn't want to imprison me there if I change my mind, and a man has got a mind to change if he so wishes you understand. You women do not have the monopoly on that one, as fanciful as you are." He grinned at her, a warm, friendly grin that showed her he meant no offence by his comments.

"Well, each to their own I say. Whatever tickles your ... live and let live," she corrected herself, remembering who she was addressing.

"Don't worry your pretty little face, my dear. It takes an awful lot to upset me, wouldn't you agree Freddie?"

"For sure Father. Take no notice, he's only teasing you. It's just his way. It will get him into really deep water one day."

With that Freddie gave the priest another mighty push. Righting himself once more, Father Sebastian chased his young friend across the river towards the cascading fall and promptly rugby tackled him full pelt into its babbling depths. Their screams of delight were drowned by the torrent from above.

She looked away and then, sensing the lateness of the hour and not wishing to intrude any longer, she waded over, back to the bank and the horses. She stroked them and peered over their warm necks of at the men playing and the fall. The sun had moved now and she could clearly see the Angel looking across the river, wings outstretched as though she were protecting it. The scene was beautiful to behold, truly a wonder.

"Hey," called Freddie. "Aren't you going to wait for me?"

"It's fine, really. Actually I was wondering if Father Sebastian could ride? Perhaps you could take the horses back together?"

"Nonsense. Wait there, I'm coming over," Freddie told her.

The men kissed again, seemed to say their goodbyes and went their separate ways. Freddie approached the bank, water pouring from his shorts. He helped her back up onto her horse and leapt up, effortlessly, onto his own.

"This way, my friend," he said, leading her through a glade.

"But I don't remember this way. Is it a short cut?"

"No, in fact it's the long way round. Just wait and see. You'll thank me."

With that he urged the horse into a quick trot, then a steady canter. She copied, keeping clear of the low-lying branches until they were out into an open space once more. They had arrived at a beach. It was secluded, white and possibly the most unspoilt she had visited anywhere. Turning to inspect the sea that stroked the coastline like a mother's love of her child, she watched as Freddie unleashed his mount into the surf. She saw him raise his arms above his head, shouting out for her to hurry up and ride with him. This was one of those moments she was never going to forget. Gently encouraging her horse to trot on, she realised she was going to have to be a lot more persuasive than that if she was going to catch Freddie. She gave a good hard kick behind the girth with one leg, only just keeping her balance in the saddle as she did so and the horse obliged, shooting off, its head like a cannon, back and forth, back and forth as it shot out. This mare had fire in her, that was clear, and when she reached Freddie's horse it was obvious she was the dominant mare of the two of them and probably of the herd.

"This is amazing. I love it."

"Shh, don't talk. You'll spoil it. It's magical isn't it? Really magical."

P O L O

"We've got the wind up our tail, haven't we?"

"Yep."

"Hopefully, that should help us to get there in good time, do you think?" she asked of her driver, slumped over the huge wheel of the horse trailer they were travelling in.

"Yep," replied her companion.

"Do you think we'll have a lot of good competition at the ground?" she wondered.

"Maybe," he answered, giving her a sideways look, momentarily. It was going to be a long journey.

"The ponies are playing up a bit in the back aren't they?" she pointed out.

"It's always the same one. They should quit soon," he said, not very reassuringly. Then he used the double de-clutch to hammer home the gears and crank the vehicle up and down the road. The horses banged against the trailer walls and no doubt each other, whinnying in the process. There was a scream of sorts from one of them and an almighty thud, which shuddered the driver's cab.

"Shit," he shouted. "I'll have to pull over."

They came to a halt and he jumped down from the driver's seat, out onto the hot dry road beneath. She watched in the wing mirrors as he disappeared around the back and out of sight. The next thing there was a second vehicle and she recognised Tom. They were talking amongst themselves, but she couldn't make out what they were saying, except for the frequent swearing and hand gestures. They seemed to be opening up the back of the trailer and she could just see Tom stretching a leg up and reaching to pull himself in.

"Give me a hand with this one. The stupid damn horse has only gone and cut its leg. You're no good to us today like that now are you, you dumb animal. Come on. Get up there," Tom ordered the ponies.

She saw the butt of a glowing cigarette fly out the back and land on the road, rolling along and under a passing truck.

"Shit, he's really hurt himself this time. I thought Michael had sorted things."

"Nope. Too drunk still from last night, the fool" said Tom disgustedly.

Just then Michael pulled up behind Tom's car, together with his truckload of polo ponies. She found herself feeling quite warm. He looked really quite sexy in that red checked shirt, his sunglasses and blonde floppy hair.

"What's wrong?" asked Michael.

"It's that dumb pony of yours, Michael. Have you seen what he's done to himself now? Get up here and look at this mess and bring something to sort his leg out, you big drunk," boomed Tom.

"Yeah, alright." Let's have a look at the shit," said Michael in reply.

She sat there in the cab wondering whether or not to try to interfere. She knew how Michael would be handling those ponies and she knew she disagreed with him. So why was her backside glued so securely to that seat? Why did she find all of these self-assured, arrogant, sexist, aggressive, belligerent men so hard to approach? She smiled to herself. She eventually plucked up the guts to see if she could be of any use to them. Perhaps pour them each a nice cup of something from the flask, make small talk about how interesting the clouds looked that day. She felt her confidence rising. After all, ponies weren't cheap. She knew that. Then there was the loss of earning from the time they were each taking off from their respective farms and the respect they stood to win or lose on the polo fields.

Suddenly, the driver's door flew open. Her driver climbed up again, grabbed his tobacco with one hand, whilst turning on the engine with the other and off they went. It was incredible how he was capable of rolling a cigarette one-handedly. Incredible to her anyway.

"Alright?" he enquired.

"Yes, thanks," she answered politely.

"Are the ponies okay now?" she wondered addressing the side of his face as he attempted to seal the cigarette paper with his tongue and keep half an eye on the road.

"Yep. Let's hope so. Michael has taken his idiot horse on his trailer. That should sort things."

"Will we miss the first game?" she asked.

"Not if I can help it, we won't. In any case you're going to have to get a move on when we do arrive - to make sure you've got Tom's ponies ready in time. Mine will be there for me by now," he said matter-of-factly.

She sat up in her seat as though the action of doing that would get them there that much faster. God, she had so much to do. She started to get a system in her head that she had learnt, working through the ponies, as and when Tom needed them. Bandages and tail, numnah, saddle, bridle, away. Hose them down, tether to trailer, next.

Back on the farm in Tamauri, she didn't need to try to keep herself busy. With polo practices, matches and tournaments, she needed to be on her toes to get the ponies fit and their tack clean and ready. It was a constant turn around. Fortunately, she had cleaned out and tidied up the tack room, so there was some order in her working life in that respect.

Following their behaviour down in Wamawatungi, she and Tom, her boss, kept their distance between each other. For him, that seemed to keep his life nice and simple. For her, it was torture. Actually, she felt she hadn't completely humiliated herself with him. In fact, she had even learnt a thing or two and that included things to do around his farmstead too. She had helped to dock the lambs tails and tag their ears. Then when Tom had to take some of his heifers to market, she had really got her hands dirty in lending a hand to load them up on his truck. She had surprised herself at how confident and strong she could be. The reality check came though when she had to be persuasive with people, men in particular. The animals she could handle. Some she clearly enjoyed working with more than others. Since the age of four, she knew she had a love of horses, so no problems there, aside from her capabilities as a horsewoman. The sheep, well it was clear they really do follow each other, which made for an easier time of it.

She remembered one time in Tamauri when she was out on one of the polo ponies, the grey, checking the sheep to see if any had cast themselves. As far as she understood things, this would be a regular episode just before they were due to be sheared, as their wool would become quite heavy, also if they were relatively heavily pregnant too. She would occasionally have to hop down off the pony and heave the animal back up, off its side and back onto its four feet again. This time it was a lamb which needed her help. It seemed somehow detached from the rest of the flock. She had been told about the orphaned lambs and how the farmers would try various ways to get one of the ewes to accept the poor animals, as one of their own. Sometimes they would take the skin from a dead lamb and drape it or tie it onto the back of the fleece of an orphan in an effort to get the grieving ewe to accept the orphan as his own. She had thought at first this was quite abysmal, but she came to see things their way. They were only trying to do the right thing. They did have some feelings for their stock, after all, some more than others, but it was a business all the same.

She helped out as best she could in the shearing shed with the sheep too. She worked as a rousier, bringing a sheep from a holding pen to one of the shearers to work on. Then she would have to shunt the wool off the floor and down to the tables where she or someone else would grade it according to its worth. Some time was spent grading and packing the wool down into these vast sacks. She would have to climb up and into them and literally scrunch the wool down with her farming boots on, to squeeze in as much as possible.

It was stinking hot in the wool shed. They all mucked in. Taking welcome breaks every two or three hours, when she would eat and take on as much fluid as the men. Well, she was doing men's work after all! Occasionally, one of the shearers she was working with would nick the ear of a sheep and blood would spurt everywhere, all over its head and face, tarnishing the fleece about the shearer's feet. Perhaps this would mean the wool wouldn't be worth as much? She didn't have the energy to ask at the time. Anyway, the shearer's concentration was wholly on the task at hand. They didn't need some pipsqueak like her, some fly by night, to irritate and annoy them any more than that sweat box of a factory was already. They had hundreds of sheep to get through and that was only the half of it. When they were done here they would be needed in another hot and sticky shearing shed or another farm, somewhere. They took their skills and their tools with them and that was that.

She learnt, astonishingly, the same barn she was working in, doubled up as a venue for the families birthday parties and pretty much any celebration going. It made financial sense and, when they had an indoor barbeque in there to celebrate the end of the busiest period of the year, she joined them in there and loved every minute of it. She couldn't tell if it was because they had made such an effort to decorate the place so well or because the hard work was at last complete, but she felt she deserved to be there enjoying the use of the place for a change. These were fond, proud memories. She was doing all right.

The other times that she felt she had a place with them was at the practice games or at least at the end. When, and especially if, she had done a good job with the tack and the ponies and particularly if Tom had won a game, she felt she could relax a little. So long as everything had been done, the rugs hanging out to dry, the ponies hosed down and tethered to the side of the trailer, she would make her way over to some of the other grooms. Tom's sister would often come over, always with a smile, no matter what the outcome. She could ride, but she wasn't all that interested in the game. They came to have an understanding, with regard to Tom and became very close friends. She learnt a lot about the relationships between the various people she had met and befriended, or tried to befriend. This whole episode for in Tamauri was a revelation for her. She felt she grew up a little as a consequence.

The time came, when the teams had practised as much as time would allow, before the polo season had really begun and

Tom and his brother Michael had their first game. That was when things really started cooking. During one of the warm-up games, Michael's pony seemed to be playing up. She had only recently mastered a slow trot with this one and admired anyone's skill if they could get more out of the animal than that. Although, evidently it was down to her own lack of skill, more than any spite the pony had in it. This was evident now, with the pony tossing its head about in the air, mouth open, teeth apart, aghast at how it was being handled. They were playing, weren't they? It was only meant to be a game, Sport. But the manner in which Michael was rough-handling him was shocking.

She had found a relatively comfortable spot to sit for a minute, on the door of a horse trailer, dropped down on the floor as a ramp for the ponies. Indulging herself in a relaxing conversation with another girl there, who was a local and able to fill her in with the goings on, present, past and future tense, she half watched. Then as it became apparent that Michael wasn't happy with his steed, she began to look towards the field with at first more interest and then with alarm. By now the pony was rearing up and sitting almost, on its back legs, which were bent, trying to contain the pressure of the weight on them. Michael was coping with bravado with the predicament he was in, at least initially. He must have been all too aware of the number of eyes on him. There was quite a crowd there. Not to mention everyone and himself included were keen to get on with the day's play. It was hotting up and the beer couldn't be kept cool for ever.

Maybe that's what did it for Michael. The thought of that pony trying its damndest to spoil things for him, again. He always seemed to be lumbered with the spooky ones or the green ones - those not up to his high expectations. She looked on, now standing, hoping Michael wouldn't lose it with the pony and in that moment he did. Taking his polo stick up in the air, a now standing Michael, side on and at the pony's head, swung his stick up and across the face of the pony. The contact sounded not dissimilar to that between stick and ball, but the effect was sickening and horrendous. The pony reared up again and with the pain and the shock fell sideways all at once. But with Michael grabbing a stronghold on the reins, there was no escaping another blow from the stick and a third and fourth. By now she was not only up on her feet but standing on the side line, toes poking over the chalk dust, like some desperate sprinter, keen to be given the 'off' and leaning into the field ready to pounce on Michael. She was so self-conscious, so aware she didn't really belong and there had been all those goings on with Tom as well. There she was witnessing this repulsive act of animal cruelty and not even looking as though she was going to even try to put an end to it.

After the fourth blow, either Michael lost his nerve with all those eyes on him or ran out of strength to hold a now frantic animal more than twice his weight, and carry on hammering in to the thing. Somehow they came to a stop. Incredibly, Michael still appeared to have a hold of the reins, just so the pony still wasn't free of him. To her further astonishment he then clambered back on to the pony's back and proceeded to get back into his position ready to take a penalty.

The game continued and progressed to some end, she could not tell what. For the rest of the game she imagined she could hear various conversations going on about her, the flirting, the teasing, the jokes, everything but a mention of that despicable behaviour earlier. She would never forget that she stood there in front of that scene and did absolutely nothing to help that pony. What was she?

Later that night back at the house and lying in her own bed, alone, she felt her head fill with those solitary thoughts. The should-have-dones, the but-whys. There was no possibility of making amends. She told herself if it happened again, she would take that stick from Michael and wrap it around his head for him. Truthfully, she was intimidated by him and knew she had seen him mistreating this pony and others before this time and still she did nothing. Hot-headed allegedly. That's what his family and friends said of Michael, not that they could possibly have meant that being that way gave him some excuse for this sort of behaviour. The pony wasn't all that different either. They were separated only by the fact no one had mistreated or abused Michael, at least, not that she was aware of.

There was more going on than just the polo that day and Michael's behaviour, surprisingly, was not the worst either. In a horse box some distance from where she had set up the ponies she was working with, one of the grooms was supposedly re-acquainting herself with an English player, in some style too by all accounts. He had done pretty well for himself back home and with some family money and enough encouragement, had his own polo team and the means to compete with them too. There was never any real money to make from these matches, so it was really and truly just an expensive hobby.

The horsebox was shifting and rocking slightly, from side to side. So gently it wasn't really all that noticeable at first and one of the other voyeurs had pointed it out for her with a smirk and a wink. A little later, she was walking one of the ponies over to a hose, set up to the side and slightly behind the same vehicle. She hadn't really thought about the two inhabitants of it very much, not wanting to get behind in her work and, in addition, wanting to give them what little privacy they could afford, in such a public place.

There were sounds all about her. The ponies snorting as the afternoon heat dried up the sandy dust about them and it was kicked up into their faces as the games went on. The hooves pounding down the field after the ball and victory in one direction, then rapidly and thunderously back up to the other end. The polo sticks clashing and the regular wallop of ball coming together haphazardly with a stick and flying up or across the game. Players and ponies alike heaving, rapid breathing, groaning, moaning, screams of agony as ponies collided with balls, sticks, each other, riders. Then the thud, crunch of a player falling from his mount and under another player's pony. Thankfully, there were no casualties on the field that day, they were all sensible enough to wear helmets at least.

In the horse box beside her and the pony she held with one hand by its reins and the hose, she could hear murmurs and desperation in a voice that seemed to almost be squeaking in a muffled, somewhat frightened way. She was too far away to peer through any cracks, so she strained her ears and neck to see if they might finish whatever they were doing in there and emerge, all well with the world. After a few minutes she turned the pony back towards the direction of the trailer and the others, where more work awaited her, readying the next pony for another chukka. Just as they were side on to the noises she had been trying to comprehend and wondering if she really was so naïve, she caught a glimpse of something sordid and frightening. The English player had this young female groom pinned against a partition within the horse box, a large, dirty hand about her mouth, the other hand down somewhere out of sight and the two of them were standing there facing her, his stomach pressed tight against the groom's back, hers against the partition. There wasn't enough to see to make out clearly and with clarity, precisely what was happening in there. But the hand over the mouth, smothering the fear and the wide, desperate eyes of the groom explained precisely enough for her what was afoot.

As she hurriedly tacked up the next pony requested of her by Tom and turned, her head spinning out of control at what her senses were telling her, she caught another glimpse of the same groom. The girl looked across, from a head hung low, her arms wrapped around herself and stooping in her gait slightly, then held a single finger to her pursed lips and carried on.

Apparently the groom in question had an issue with her visa and was home within the week. Best place for her, no doubt.

Amazingly, undeterred by all this, she found herself back in the swing of things, at least when it came to the social side of life around the polo scene. It was particularly easy to accomplish this when she was steeped in alcohol in copious quantities, and largely in the form of Vodka Mules. Failing that, beer, cider, lager, wine. Pretty much anything to relax her body after a gruelling shift with the ponies, the sheep, the men and likewise her mind.

There were many episodes when she found herself prostrate on the ground, in some paddock somewhere on the farm in Tamauri. Largely speaking, this would have followed from a fall from one of the ponies. One accident in particular stayed with her as a very lucky escape, in terms of her physical well-being at least. It involved the grey, with whom at this stage she believed she had conquered her nerves, probably even her fears over riding her. Now, she felt confident to take her out alone, away from the other ponies, in order to check the sheep and lambs.

It was on one of these occasions previously that she had discovered a lamb by itself, possibly orphaned. She tried to persuade it to join the rest of the flock but it looked weak and anyway, the others didn't appear to want to accept this outcast. Instead, she took the initiative, her heart getting the better of her for a change. With the surprisingly heavy lamb in her arms and trusting with all her might that the grey wouldn't take it upon herself to bolt off back to her mates tethered beside the tack room, she somehow managed to lift the animal over the saddle. It was a huge effort and unfortunately didn't seem to be sufficient for the lamb to remain safely in place. Probably owing to the fact the poor animal was incapable of holding on in any shape or form. Eventually, she chose to carry the lamb in her arms, the reins looped over her hand and resting on her wrist, so that if the grey spooked at something it saw unexpectedly - like a piece of wool blowing in the wind, which was highly likely given it was normally prevailing in this corner of the farm, she and the lamb would stand no chance whatsoever. In spite of this she got the three of them safely back. Un-tacked the grey, walked with the lamb for a further ten minutes to the house, prolonged by the fact she was exhausted by now, what with the lamb starting to feel like a dead weight and her arms losing virtually all feeling. Even so, they were there standing in the porch-way, all the family who were around coming out to look at them.

The response was a mixed bag of impressiveness and dismissiveness. The former from the women-folk and Scott. The latter from Tom and especially Michael, who was almost laughing at her in ridicule. He told her in no uncertain terms she ought to have left the lamb to cope by itself, because it wasn't worth a thing to them in its present state. She was already feeling silly, even ashamed of her ignorance until Scott gave her one of his smiles and took her to one side. He placed the lamb gently in the cottage garden, which took up one side of the grounds about the house. Then he reassured her they might well be able to get a little for the animal and more generously still promised she could have whatever they made for it.

As it turned out, they made sufficient for the lamb to secure her the funds for a pair of rather elegant looking evening shoes. Good job too, since at the end of the polo season she had been told of a Ball or a party at least, to which she would be invited. Now, all she had to find was a dress.

This time around though her travels with the grey pony had led her a merry dance and that was certainly no lie. Just as she was starting to feel like a regular cowgirl, sitting pretty in that saddle, or so she felt, well no-one else was there to boost her ego. Then it happened. Suddenly the pony beneath her started to freak out somewhat, as she was known to. She let out a few snorts, then was pitter-pattering about on her hooves. She was told that polo ponies could turn on a penny. She was so agile on her legs. Very useful in a match, no doubt, but now, there stood a number of fences between them and the tack room, where the remaining ponies were waiting for their return. Frighteningly, that return came about all too quickly. The pony had begun to pace around now, impatiently, irritated perhaps. In any case she had made a decision to stop work for the day and head home, or at least back for some equine company. She tried to calm her down, and herself into the bargain. Anyone who is worth their salt when it comes to horses, ponies and temperamental, strong-minded polo ponies will tell you, if the animal you're holding chooses to bolt, you had better sit tight for the ride.

Remembering all this, she believed, she was doing precisely that. For a second or two, she sort of went with the flow, as it were. Pretending to herself, and hopefully fooling the pony, that she was in control. She knew exactly what she was doing and the pony was purely going in the direction she meant her to go in the first place! So much so, though, that when they did hit the first fence, that was just what they did.

She had absolutely no knowledge of the pony flaying herself against the barbed wire. In actual fact she hadn't even been aware the wire was rigged up on that lower level of the fencing in the paddock. The next thing she knew of herself was sort of seeing the top of the fence and hedge, then the sky, some herringbone clouds, across a rather stunning backdrop of a distant mountain range, which stood like some grey and white dinosaur adjacent to the farm. Finally, smack down on to her back. Bang! Her back had come into contact with a random stone, which just so happened to have left itself marginally to the side of where her unprotected head was going to come to a halt. Could have been worse then.

The very first thing she thought was how utterly stupid she had been not to have worn a regular safety features-laden, kite-marked riding helmet. The latest variety too and not the old style, attractive though they may be, black velvet type. She still had a couple of those knocking around useless, back home in England. Precious good they were doing to her now. They never fitted correctly anyway, since she had found both in a charity shop somewhere. You get what you pay for. How true was that.

The second thought that irritated her, was the realisation that the whole episode might well have been watched, witnessed. It was a strong possibility that Michael might have driven past at just that moment. He would surely have a field day over this.

Ridiculously, the last thing she was concerned about was her back. But then as she carefully went to raise herself up from that punishing dry, hard sun-baked earth, peppered with crusty sheep dung and almost blistering in the heat, she thought for a terrible moment, when is it going to hurt? She was certainly able to get to her feet, though she was frightening herself with the idea that maybe her spinal cord was going to tear with the slightest move, the next move perhaps? Shaking now and in a daze. Not knowing what to do. Where was the pony? She had responsibilities for the ponies. What if Michael had seen it all? What if anyone had seen?

Then, to her relief, it was Scott who approached her with a sensitive, concerned, fatherly look about his weather-beaten features. He held a hand out and seeing up close that she was standing, able to walk, that much was clear, he gave her one of his unique smiles. She managed something similar in return. Noticing his car parked ad hoc, just behind him, she started to piece together that he must have driven across country in what was genuinely a town car. Over that hard, bumpy, gravelled soil, then left it side on, door still open in his haste to reach her.

There was a period of forgetfulness, understandable really. Then they were back at the house in the kitchen. Tom, Michael and virtually everyone in their family had got the gist of what had transpired. They were all keeping to themselves as men do sometimes. Watching on. Waiting. Scott and the women-folk took the initiative. They began to ask the obvious, expected questions of what hurt and what could she move and then someone was on the phone.

They certainly took care of her. She had appointments set up for x-rays. Then when they were clear, physiotherapy for as long as she would need it for a sprained lumbar region.

As for Tom, he wasn't about to have a kindly discussion with her about her job prospects with him. What she did learn of his intentions, with regard to her post, she heard from his sister. He had been advised by a friend and a fellow polo player to tell her to pack her things and get herself back to England post haste. After all she wasn't much use to him in her state, was she?

P O L O
T H E   R E V E L A T I O N

"How's it going?" she asked after the two girls.

"Good, thanks. How are you? How are the ponies and Tom? I hope he's treating you better now," one friend enquired in their usual, sincere and concerned way.

"Yep, good, good, good. Actually, things are going pretty smoothly at the moment. Mustn't grumble, you know."

She brushed off the friendly intrusion into her life with Tom. Even though his sister had every right to know, she felt she ought to try to retain some privacy between herself and her boss and any relationship they had going on between them. Somehow it helped her hold onto her self-respect a little. But just as she was feeling good about herself, Tom's sister enlightened her some more as to exactly what kind of history he had with a previous groom of his.

"They used to be an item," she almost blurted out, if she hadn't had her head bent down and her voice in a whisper. There must have been a look of puzzlement on her face, because the friend went on in greater detail.

"The groom over there. You know, the one working up at Pagets. She used to be Tom's groom before you arrived. They had quite a long relationship, for Tom anyway. Mum and Dad thought they were going to become engaged at one stage. Tom even borrowed some money from them and everyone was sure he was going to produce a ring."

"What happened to the money then? What did he use it for?" she wondered, rather irrelevantly and quite preposterously really, considering she knew and her friends knew it was Tom she was interested in, not his finances.

"Oh, he had a few pieces of farming machinery he hadn't finished paying for, on hire purchase. Mum told him he was a fool. She's a hard-working girl, who knows her stuff."

Well, that had been all too clear to her. What was more irritating was the way this old flame of Tom's, groom, whatever she was just simply got on with it too, never seeming to brag or show off. Worst still, whenever she wasn't able to manage something herself, like the time on the polo field when Tom wanted her to try a different style of bridle on one of the ponies. She could tell by his manner that he was in no mood for any bother. She was expected just to knuckle down, clueless or not. Tom was still perched up on his mount, like one of those greats - Alexander or Troy or someone - lording it up, God-like, glaring down at her and over his shoulder as his pony pivoted around in anticipation of getting back into the game. He looked across at his old hand and lover and muttered something to her between smiles and knowing looks of secret and special times spent together. Then he spun his face back to his ludicrously inept English protégée. He virtually spat out an order to her to let his obviously favoured ex-groom lend a hand and explain how the tack went. Then away they went, horse and rider, back into the game once more, stick in hand swinging a full three-sixty and swiping the dry, parched ground in the process.

"She might not be a pretty face, but she's a worker" she continued.

"It's her twenty-first next weekend. Everyone is going. You'll be invited." She told her.

She wasn't too certain if she wanted to be invited, yet this ex-groom had been nothing but friendly and helpful.

"Watch yourself, though. There's more to her and Tom than you realise," she went on.

"But there's nothing between them now, is there?" She asked Tom's sister hopefully.

"Oh, you're too nice! There's always going to be something going on between those two. She can't resist him and he can't say no to sex, whenever he can get it. He's a man, remember," came the explanation.

Nope, she definitely hadn't spotted that one. As far as she was aware, theirs was a platonic, mutually respectful friendship - a working partnership. How stupid she was. When she had just begun to believe there was a glimmer of hope for some sort of long-lasting relationship and settlement between herself and Tom. Now his sister and her mate stood there, telling her she had got everything the wrong way round, upside down, topsy-turvy, confused. Yes, she was that all right. Although with these facts she wasn't altogether convinced, she needn't be too mixed-up any more; she could start afresh. A working friendship purely and simply with Tom and who knows with everyone else, well of the male variety anyway, but who could tell what the future would hold for her? Maybe Tom didn't know what he wanted? Perhaps he couldn't see that it was her he needed all along. She could live with that. She smiled at her friend, raised a beer to her in appreciation of her candour and took a long, hard suck.

BIRTHDAY CELEBRATIONS

She walked into the hall as confidently as she could for someone who was infatuated with a man who didn't seem to give a monkeys about her. To lower her self-esteem even further, her rival was hanging off his arm in a white dress that mimicked a bridal gown and Tom didn't seem to be able to take his eyes off her. Not to mention her ample breasts, both of which she noted were annoyingly pert for a girl her size.

"Here's a drink, mate," Tom's sister declared, pushing a glass into her hand. She didn't say so but they realised it was clear she needed some Dutch courage.

"He's not worth it," came the dreaded cliché.

"Well, unfortunately for me, I think he is. I wish I didn't, but there you have it." There it was then, the truth. Though she still wasn't certain lust was playing a bigger part in all this than love.

"Listen, you're a good friend. I'm going to tell you this for your own good. Tom is like a sailor; he has a girl in every port. She doesn't know it, or if she does she's a bigger fool than him, but every time he's overseas you can bet he's got someone to keep him warm at night. There's a woman in Germany, a player and sponsor apparently. Anyway, when he's not pandering to her every whim, largely to seal a deal with her to help keep up his expensive habits, he's shacked up with her daughter! In all this the daughter helps him out with the ponies in her school holidays. So, he's got them all exactly where he wants them and the mother is paying him for the privilege! Now, that can't be right, can it?"

"Has there been anyone he has truly cared for, you know, treated properly?" She pushed for more information or perhaps ammunition on Tom.

"Yes. There was and still is just the one girl for Tom. He fell in love with another English girl. She worked here for him as a groom a long, long time before you came here. She's back home now, but not before Tom proposed to her. She denied him her hand in marriage at first, blaming her young age and a desire to go to university, but she never went. When her visa ran out again she used that as another excuse to escape this second show of his commitment. She yo-yos back and forth when she can get her papers sorted. I know there's no bad feelings or ill intent there on her part, but she taunts him all the same. I'm sure we haven't seen the last of her. She was lovely; such a happy, friendly, bubbly girl. We all miss her," she ended sadly.

But she wanted to know more, know everything. So it wasn't a culture thing, no nationality issue that was coming between her and Tom. His heart wasn't for the taking. He had given it away, two or three times over. He was hollow. There was nothing to him, no substance, no love in that fit, sun-kissed body of his. Frustration, hurt, confusion; that was all that he had in him now. If he was going to show any attempt at some demonstration of affection for anyone other than his mystery groom from England, who preceded herself, it was all fake. He was a fraud.

"Do you think she will ever say yes?"

"Who knows. He's such a dark one, not even Mum knows what makes him tick sometimes. He's in her good books for now. Partly, because it's a busy time of year and he knows his father might lend him some kit for his farm during harvesting, if he creeps around them long enough. Oh listen to me. I'm turning into such a cynic! But you can hopefully see how things are pieced together for him now. He's a user, a womaniser, a shark. Yes, I know he's my brother but sometimes I'm so ashamed of him. He treats you appallingly, everyone can see that. We're only surprised you haven't left already!" she finished.

"My God! I, I thought he ......" she petered off, believing she was better off keeping her astonishment of Tom's past and present capabilities to herself. She thought if she held it together, as if she knew all this about Tom already and now so much was known of the goings-on between him and her, perhaps his family and friends would carry on in the knowledge she was all right? This was one of those moments in her life that would stand out in her memory for a long time to come. As a poignant image of her as one human being who could stand up for their actions, for themselves even. She knew then, in that response she gave, she was telling them Tom meant everything to her but she was going to have to accept the truth, she meant nothing to him. They linked arms, like girlfriends do sometimes, as comrades fighting the good fight together and glared across at Tom and his cronies.

At that moment Tom took it upon himself to make a grand announcement. It came in two parts, one following the other in such close succession that she could barely take it all in.

"Thanks to everyone for coming to help us celebrate twenty-one wonderful and fun-filled years in the life of this fine upstanding figure of a woman I hold before you," he began.

She had no idea he could have such a way with words. Couldn't he have found such eloquence for the times he spent in her company, specifically when they were sharing the heat of his bed sheets between their respective thighs? How revolting was she, how jealous. She felt childish again and took another long draft of wine she was cradling to help her feel a grown-up again. It didn't, only serving to fire up the envy she felt towards this local farm girl. There was worse yet.

"We have another reason why we have asked you all to join us, haven't we, darling?" he declared.

It was altogether too sickening for her, but compelling at the same time. What was he going to say next, what announcement, what revelation did he want to share?

"Somehow we have managed to keep this from you all, well almost all of you," he started.

A look was shared between Tom and his best mate. The same man whom she had come to dislike for reasons she could not tell. He in turn had been standoffish and very false around her, busting a gut to find anything halfway pleasant to say to her. She watched the way Tom was behaving around his girl. He seemed to really care. She remembered how he could be.

"The fact of the matter is, I have asked this lovely lady ..... to do me the honour ....."

No, no, don't say the obvious. Please don't say those words when we all know what's coming.

" ...... to be my wife ... and ... and," he tried to say above the din of the applause and screaming approval, " ... and ..."

At this point he had taken himself around the back of his fiancée and with one hand on her shoulder, the other began to rotate about the small mound which comprised her stomach and evidently a little more.

"... the mother of our unborn child."

More clapping, foot stomping and general raising of the roof.

Shit! How bad could things be? She had been bitching inwardly that the white dress was doing nothing to hide that bulge she had got for herself. And whilst she had been assuming it was too much beer and an evident disliking for healthy food, all along her archenemy was shielding the most beautiful precious thing, life itself. With this thought she felt ashamed. Good luck to her; she would need it by all accounts. Suddenly this rival didn't seem so threatening anymore. She looked bewildered, possibly a little scared. It wasn't the first time she had seen another side to someone out here that wasn't paraded for all to see at first glance. Perhaps we were all like ducks or swans, according to how blessed we were at birth, but incidentally still all gliding through life on the surface, disguising the reality beneath.

"I had no idea, honestly, absolutely no clue. They've kept that so quiet. I would have told you. Well, I suppose I probably had my suspicions, if I was honest. You have to be so careful you don't spread any gossip out here. It's such a small place. It's hard. You're such a good friend." Tom's sister wiped a tear from her friend's cheek before anyone else saw.

"Don't let them get to you. You're better than that. Show him you don't care what he does, whose heart he breaks, so long as it's not yours. Come on, let's get ratted. Give me your glass. I'll get us a refill. I reckon we deserve it, after that outburst, don't you?"

"No, you're right. Life's too short and all that. I know it gets to them if you look as though you're having a great time without them... I'll try," she added in agreement.

Three long, arduous weeks passed following that party and then she learnt the engagement had been called off. Allegedly, Tom's foolery in Europe had even him sailing too close to the wind for comfort. He had taken a tumble in a practice game, suffered mild concussion and ended up in the local hospital. Apparently, one of the staff treating him knew his fiancée. Having worked out what his hidden agendas were out there, she had felt obliged to semi break the confidentiality code and tell all. The sweet revenge certainly came delivered as a dish best served cold. Tom's bride-to-be told him the baby wasn't his. In fact, she didn't know whose it was, allegedly. It didn't make her feel any better or worse, she was indifferent if she felt anything. She wasn't about to become a gossipmonger - but hey, it made life quite interesting at times! She wondered if Tom's fiancée would go through with the pregnancy. Wasn't there a film she saw once, where the cheated wife dumps her adulterous husband, but then goes on to become all chummy with his lover right up to the point where she is there for her at the birth of her illegitimate child? She fantasised for a minute or so that she could do that for another person, to be so selfless. No, she couldn't.

TRAVELS
WITH MY COMPANION

"You do realise, if you don't get your arse into gear and get back up in the saddle for him, Tom is going to tell you to go back home," he warned.

She gasped. She hadn't realised things were that bad. As far as she was concerned, Tom was moody but otherwise as sorry and sympathetic as a boss could be that their employee was out of action.

"Right. Well, I guess I had better get on with it."

"Well, yes, if you still want your job, you have," he explained.

Putting it in such simple terms, yet making her realise that was why she was out there, to do a job, she got up and followed him out.

She liked the way he had arranged a sort of mock corral for the ponies under his care, using simple but effective knots with spare rope he had found.

"This is clever," she commented, knowing full well he was a sucker for compliments. She had to get him and keep him on her side as the only other Brit out there she had met so far.

Especially, if they were supposed to be spending Christmas together.

"Well, it does the job," he replied, grabbing a handful of lead reins and ponies in the process.

"Right, these are yours. Get up on this one. Here, I'll give you a hand." He cupped his hand for her foot and virtually threw her up onto the saddle.

"Thanks."

"Right, remember, you want to keep your job, yes? Just follow behind me, we'll take it nice and easy. If you feel unsure of yourself, slow them down again."

He was really very reassuring, caring even, a very, very likeable man. She smiled back at him as he turned and looked over his shoulder at her from his pony. They spent the rest of the warm morning exercising the ponies around the paddock there and then went in for lunch.

"What are we having then?" She asked him, feeling slightly guilty at her presumption that he would be doing the cooking.

"I've bought us a small chicken to share. The turkeys would have been far too much for us to get through," he said.

"Can I do anything?" She offered.

"Pour us both a drink, if you like. There are some bottles in that bag on the floor there by the fridge," he explained to her. She turned around and spotted the white carrier bag half split open at one side where a pack of four had stretched its use over and above the limits of its supposed weight load. She peered inside. There was a litre bottle of Bombay gin, a Chardonnay and a bottle of fizz.

"What will you have?" She asked him.

"I'll go for a gin and tonic. Look in the fridge, towards the back, you should see some tonic water and there's ice in the freezer compartment. No lemon though, that would be sacrilege with that gin!"

She found what he'd asked for and having located a tumbler, proceeded to concoct a gin and tonic for her friend.

"There you go," she said, handing him the chilled glass.

"Happy Christmas."

"Happy Christmas." He gulped down half of the glass, holding onto it about the rim to keep the ice cold and carried on stirring the gravy.

"I'm impressed you make proper gravy," she remarked, pouring herself a beer. Even the mere smell of gin sent her heaving, ever since that experiment at boarding school.

"Why?" he responded starkly.

Not expecting his reaction, she found herself feeling agitated again. He seemed to enjoy himself with her in these stupid, ridiculous, unnecessary battles over the trivial. Christ, it was meant as a compliment, not an accusation. Then again, maybe it could have come across as somewhat patronising. She decided to smile and hope that would smooth things over between them again, certain in the knowledge he held some feelings towards her. It worked. He downed his glass, reached across the sink to the gin and poured himself another much, much larger drink.

"Here's the tonic water," she offered.

"Thanks. How's the beer?" he replied, with a little smirk.

"It's alright, but if you don't mind I'm not sure I'll finish all of it."

"Go on, you big girl," he taunted.

Well, yes alright, it was Christmas after all. She could take the teasing today of all days. It wasn't as if she could see she had much choice in the matter, what with being stuck out there, just the two of them, motorless. She took another swig and struggled to swallow the gas.

The only competition she felt she had for his affection was a local girl, well tomboy really, who seemed an expert at all things manly, including how to drive a combine-harvester. This was terribly sexist, she knew that much, but since she couldn't play this girl at her own game, when it came to machinery and farming life in general, she would have to use all her feminine wiles to win this man of men over that way instead. They sat down at right angles to each other at the kitchen table and enjoyed their festive lunch as much as their company.

"This is delicious," she exaggerated.

"It's passable," he said, modestly.

She thought to herself, again, how much this man loved himself, how extremely talented he believed himself to be. There were brighter, fitter, less arrogant men on this planet, she knew that to be a fact.

"More wine?" he offered. She nodded with a mouth full of stuffing and peas. Well, he was generous to a fault at least, she would give him that.

"You must let me do the washing up."

God, they were sounding more domesticated and married by the hour!

"No, leave that," he ordered her, almost with a snarl.

It was when he was like this, a little drunk and very macho that she wasn't entirely certain where she fitted into things. He neither made her feel welcome, not at ease anyhow, nor provided her with enough evidence as if to say he was intent on getting to know her more intimately. Men, they played such games at times.

CHRISTMAS

"I got a Christmas pudding for us to share, if you're interested," he announced.

"Oh! yum. Yes please," she said excitedly.

Too excitedly, she thought to herself with hindsight. God, she may as well have the words "I'm gagging for it," on her forehead. Yum. How ridiculous did that sound? She felt she was making such an idiot of herself.

He reappeared from the cosy little kitchen with two plates and a bottle held in position in his armpit.

"Come on then, help me with all this," he ushered her with a glint in his eye.

She hesitated as to whether to take the two plates for fear of dislodging the bottle. More champagne, she noted from the label. That was what she was really interested in. She made her mind up and reached for the bottle. He let the plates drop to the floor, grabbed her wrist with one hand and the bottleneck with the other.

"Whoops," he whispered through a look of mischief.

"Shall we open this one in my bedroom?"

She didn't have time to think, let alone answer. Although, she didn't really believe he was after one. Something more like, after the other from the look of his tight jeans. She followed his oversized backside into the room along the corridor.

It was a typical bachelor pad in a sense. Clothes sprawled all about the floor, inter-mingled with screwed-up bed sheets, an odd sock, deodorant half-hidden under the bed. On the windowsill was an ashtray, or at least the upturned lid of a jam jar, half filled with stale, yellow, tobacco-tinged water. Beside this, a bottle of champagne opened with what appeared to be the same again, as its contents. By now she felt she had seen enough to warrant an opinion that it was most certainly unlikely to be fizz - far from it. The window was open ajar, the breeze blowing one half of the tasteless, dirty curtains inwards, then sucking them out again. She wasn't sure if she fancied the bed or the floor; one thing was for definite, she fancied him. Actually, she probably could have fancied anyone or anything at that point, with all that alcohol inside her, but he would do for now.

He beckoned her to come and lie down next to him. Too slow! He was up and around the back of her next, pressing how happy he was to make her acquaintance into her upper thigh. Great! He was too drunk to hit the mark. She would play it by ear. They undressed each other more ravenously than they had devoured the chicken they had shared for lunch. It didn't matter if buttons were pulled off or shirts were torn. They had the whole place and the entire Christmas break together, with no chance of an interruption or disturbance.

He left her knickers on, which interested her. They were just about the sexiest ones she had packed for her trip, but she felt he just preferred to slip underneath the material. To feel the silk sliding up and down him. He nudged her buttocks, press, press, push and then plunged, deep, deep, deeper still inside her. Ouch, no, not there. Oh God, he's in the wrong place! She regretted not going to the bathroom after that heavy meal. Oh, please God don't let him be filthy when he came out of her again. He started to say something in her ear.

"You love it, don't you. You love it right there. Tell me you want it. Say you want it harder," he told her.

He knew exactly what he was doing. He knew all the right moves, all the places that got to her.

"Yes, yes, I want it. Harder, give it to me harder," she responded willingly to him. She was past caring now. He could please himself, just so long as he pleased her, pleasured her. She found herself thinking out loud.

"Pleasure me, do it to me."

She hardly recognised herself, her voice even. She couldn't believe he had any more in him, any more length. What a big boy. What a naughty, big boy! Again, she said what was on her mind.

"Naughty. You're very naughty," she told him.

She began to spank his rump as it raised itself, muscles taught and clenched, then down once more. He ripped himself out of her, spun her over and ducked down between her legs, pushing her legs apart in the process. She gasped as he started to lap away. Christ, she was drenched down there; sopping wet. She could hear him gulping, taking it down. It made her feel powerful, dominant. This was like payback. She placed a sweaty hand onto the top of his head, to prevent him from coming up for air.

"Yes, don't stop. There. Oh! yes, just there," she told him.

It was his turn to take the orders now. He delved into her, hungry for it. Desperate to drink each and every drop of her. He was sort of nibbling now, gnawing at her. She worried he would really hurt her. He was beginning to take charge again. No, no. She liked being over him. Wanting him to stay on the floor in front of her, submissive. Pushing him back away from her, she reached forwards to give something back to him now. He let himself be pushed around, squatting with his feet and palms placed apart and downwards, his large buttocks splayed out on the messy carpet under him. She jumped on him, licking him about his nipples, nipping at them, kissing his neck and collar bone. All of a sudden she dived down to his groin, kissing constantly, kissing all about the inside of his legs. First down a little and teasingly up, just enough until she heard him gasp and almost give up and let go entirely, but then she would move away again and still back up and all the while he was feeling warmer and sticky. She wasn't keen on the hairiness of him yet he was desperate for her and so she brushed this inconvenience aside. He was at bursting point when he took her face and raised it to his, kissing her fiercely, over and over again. Was there love between them? She wasn't convinced, yet.

"Now, just you wait there. Don't move an inch," he told her. She did as he said. He seemed to be searching under the bed and about the floor for something. He emerged with the champagne he had brought into the room earlier.

"I think you've been a bad girl," he announced emphatically.

He was right and she knew it. Outwardly, she could come across as very prudish. This was especially true if the company she was in was not familiar to her. Strangers would make her feel anxious, unsure of herself and definitely terribly uncomfortable. Inwardly though, she was a minx. An impish, filthy, dirty, cheeky, tormenting minx. In truth she liked it that way, always having the ability to surprise, shock even, when the mood took her, of course.

She found herself reaching down for his mighty length, stroking, fondling all around his taught, manly ways. She teased with her fingers and thumb about his testicles, admiring the clever way a man's body always kept those cooler than the rest of his burning torso, even now. Otherwise he was on fire.

"Wait," he hissed persuasively. They were looking directly into each other's eyes now.

"No," she said, challenging him still further and with that she pushed him backwards again then lowered her face between his bulging thighs. Taking him all up in her mouth, it was her turn to dine now. He squealed, just a little, but in stroking her hair gently she knew he was okay with everything. She wasn't surprised. She had been the first time she had tried her wickedness on an unsuspecting guinea pig, not in the literal sense of course. That time her male companion had expressed such gratitude during and afterwards that she had made a mental note for her list of do's and don'ts in the bedroom department.

She got back to concentrating on the task at hand when, wham. What the hell was he doing to her now?

"Just try to relax."

She obliged. He had taken hold of the bottle by now, opened it almost entirely with one hand, popping the cork somewhere across the mountain of pillows and chaos. Taking a good swig himself, then sharing a bubbly kiss with her, he took the remainder and tipped it all over his riving, scorching hot body, his chest arching in the process. It hit the mark and now, refreshed and with renewed strength he grasped the bottle about the neck and reached around behind her with it.

What she was experiencing now was that same specimen, which had held the fizz, searching its way into her. It felt cold at first, though hard, something she was both familiar with as well as comfortable with.

That was until he tried to ram it home harder, further, up and into her.

"Stop, stop, no, oh that's too much, no come out a bit," she yelled to him.

"Sorry, sorry. Okay, just a little then. There, how's that? Alright?" he asked after her.

"Mmm, I think so. Oh yes, mmm," she moaned manoeuvring herself into a more accommodating position for his sex toy. She wasn't thinking very clearly at this stage, hardly any thoughts at all were coming to her, only her senses, her feelings down there where he was steering her with that empty bottle of Moet-et-Chandon. Gushing with the sensation of it, she believed she must have been capable of re-filling the vessel.

Not totally immune to improvising with any marginally phallic-looking tool that came to hand for herself in her time, she couldn't feel too horrified now. What disturbed her slightly was how or what he was making of her? She opened her eyes for a moment in an effort to read his mind. Thankfully, he too was in the throws of everything. Jaw tilted back, revealing his pulsing veins, mouth apart, ever such a little, so that she caught a glimpse of his teeth and the glistening redness of his tongue.

"Kiss me," she asked him.

He obliged and withdrew the redundant champagne. He pulled her straight down and onto him. Her black hair fell forward and broke up on his shoulders and neck, like a gentle summer wave being tugged back by the moon.

"Urghh!" he groaned through gritted teeth now.

Tossing her hair about her face and forcing his fingers into her mouth and about her wet lips. He clutched her hips and levered her weight up and crashing down onto himself over and over, as a ship in a storm. Then at precisely the moment she was screaming at him not to stop they collided together and climaxed in a frenzy of juices. No longer simply moist, they were saturated. Their liquids mingled as one, slipping out of her and trickling over him. They collapsed in a pile, as messy, and rancid now as the matter they shared began to congeal, like the room they had abused.

She woke with a start, jolting his heavy torso in the process and awakening him from his perfect slumber.

"Sorry," she apologised.

"What time is it?" he asked himself, twisting his wrist over to read his watch.

"What does it say?" she wondered in a daze.

"It's still Christmas, just," he replied.

"I've got a little something for you," he said.

"Oh, nothing new there then," she teased.

"Ha! Ha! You wish," he responded and rolled her off himself.

He was always getting one up on her. Smarty pants.

Disappearing again, back into the kitchen he returned to discover she had managed to raise enough energy to leave their pit also. He found her sprawled across the sofa watching some late night rubbish. He noticed her chest was still heaving and lent over the back of her, planting a warm hand down over a breast and around her nipple. It stood proud and erect. Tweaking it between thumb and index finger, he squeezed a touch harder testing her nerve.

"Ouch!" she called in protest and grabbed his hand, kissing him about his wrist.

"What's this rubbish you've got on?" he enquired, raising his face up to the box.

"My thoughts exactly. Switch it over, can you?"

"Come on. We've got to get some shuteye. Early start tomorrow. I'm just going to check the ponies."

"Fine, fine, fine. Sleep well," she told him. She wondered why she had said that, after all wasn't she going to be sharing his bed for the night? Then she recalled the quagmire of sex juices, alcohol and sweat they had walked away from so unashamedly. On second thoughts perhaps they should kip down in their respective beds? She didn't trust herself not to sprawl all over him at some point in the early hours. It was always the same, a good nap of sufficient length, enough to get her hot, young, virile blood up again and she was the horny devil once more. No, they had a long drive up the east coast and beyond at sunrise. Knowing she in no way fancied taking over any one moment of the driving, the least she could offer him was good company, hangover into the bargain to boot.

Heaving herself up from the furniture and prizing her stinging eyes from that goggle box, she shuffled away to another bedroom at the back of the house, behind the kitchen. Walking through, past the heap of unwashed plates and dishes, a guilty feeling welled up inside her. What a sight. She was in no state to deal with it now. Christ, she was still physically shaking after that ordeal with him.

She lay down, shattered. Her vagina was burning after his presence and everything else she had agreed to let him try with her. It was comforting in a way, like a type of punishment for the wicked things they had done to each other. Still feeling restless, she knelt up in the bed and held the curtain back to peer outside. There he was, throwing rugs over the ponies, a cigarette glowing fiercely in his mouth as he drew in. One or two of the ponies snorted, another tripped slightly. All done, he turned to walk back into the house raising a hand to bid her goodnight, acknowledging her attention without even the need to look up. It was as if he gained another sense, an awareness, an intuition. Maybe, it was the connection he had with the ponies that brushed off when he was in the company of people he was familiar with, and my God was he familiar with her.

BOXING DAY

She awoke to the sound of hooves, clambering up the ramp into the back of the trailer.

"Come on then," he called to the other ponies, as they ambled across from the far side of their paddock. They knew precisely what was going on, but in the morning's searing heat the shade of the tree, where they had slept for the night, seemed too much of a relief to leave.

She watched him at work, whilst squeezing a sweater over her head. Forgetting herself for a moment, she tugged it off again and flitted her eyes about the room for her bra. It was mingling with somebody else's scrunched up laundry and smelt of the same person's body odour. Discarding it, she grabbed a short-sleeved shirt instead and tied the pullover about her waist over her shorts and brown leather belt.

He was up in the horse trailer now, tethering the ponies for the journey across to a neighbouring stud for their own festive break. A friend there had agreed to watch out for them whilst he was off gallivanting, sightseeing and generally doing the tourist thing.

Making her way through the kitchen, towards the door, she took a backwards step beside the fridge. Half-hidden at the back was a pot of strawberry yoghurt with the added extra of some healthy grain. That sounded pretty beneficial to her. Dairy produce. A cure-all for hangovers if ever there was one. Having said that she would have preferred to have unearthed a tub of ice cream, rum and raisin, or mint-choc-chip would have sufficed. For a second she pondered as to whether or not the scuzzy occupants of the farmstead, she was guest in, continued their unsavoury habits in the food department? Pictures of furry mould of varying colours and quantities flashed in her mind's eye as she lifted the lid. It looked and, on raising it to her nose, smelt fine. She tilted the container to be certain, reading the use-by date.

Sitting down to devour it she noticed yesterday's newspaper on the chair and placed it on the table at an angle to her breakfast and settled down to a feast. The unwashed plates and other kitchen paraphernalia were still cluttering up the place. It was still only the day after Christmas; surely he wouldn't be too annoyed if she wasn't being her domesticated, conscientious usual self? Particularly given the head she had on her, next to the wonderfully satisfying service she had given him last night. There was a semi-clean spoon, which she had to hazard a guess had only been used for their pudding and started to devour the yoghurt.

There were unhappy noises coming from outside and several expletives, unbecoming even by his standards. She stood up, strawberry yoghurt still cupped in one hand, spoon brimming over with the same in the other. Peering across the yard to where he stood with one of the ponies, she strained to work out the problem, tipping the yoghurt down and over her blouse and the right leg of her shorts as she did so. She glanced down, having caught the mishap out of the corner of her eye.

"Oh great," she said out loud, annoyed with herself.

She took the spoon and attempted to scrape as much of the mess as she could, taking a damp dishcloth in an effort to remove the rest. She lifted her eyes to the yard once more, still wiping away at the material.

"Stand still," he was telling the grey. The pony he was holding with one hand on a lead rein was trying to circle him, catching its hooves as it did so.

"Come on now girl, I only want to take a look at the damage," he said patiently, although he sounded worried.

She left the remains of the yoghurt and the smeared spoon on the side, by the draining board, and filled the kettle with fresh cold water. Having plugged it in and found the switch she sidled out to see if she could be of any use?

"What's happened?" she asked.

"Oh, it's this ridiculous tailgate. It was supposed to have been fixed properly after last weekend's tournament. One of Michael's animals managed to put its leg through the planks" he informed her.

"Did it do any damage?" she said enquiringly.

"To the trailer or itself? No, it cut its fetlock pretty badly, a nasty gash right down the back of the leg there." He demonstrated for her on the grey, not wishing to assume she would know the terminology. She knew enough by then to reckon on the pony being out of action for some time to come. The Christmas holidays had come as a saving grace for that poor animal, or sure enough Michael would have made every effort to carry on riding it.

"What about this one?" she continued, looking the grey over. She caught sight of the blood around its knee, before he had a chance to answer.

"Well, you can see for yourself," he said, pointing his head in the direction of the knee and then across to the gaping hole in the tailgate.

"Same damn place. Michael obviously thought a quick cover-up job would be all right. Now there's even more work needed on it and another pony is out of action."

She could tell he was annoyed. He had taken on the responsibility for these ponies and with that came an unspoken understanding that he would be made even more welcome amongst the locals. How he was going to sort this one out, virtually single-handedly, she couldn't fathom.

Yet again, he proved himself to be resourceful.

"Can you go inside and give Tom a call? You'll find the number at the front of my Filofax," he explained.

"Where's that?" she pressed him further.

"Oh, I don't know. Look around," he exploded. There was a moment's silence. "Try on top of the television," he added, adjusting his tone.

She understood exactly why he might be feeling the pressure. Even if it was a sexist thing to imagine, she still felt she wished she was a man at that point, because perhaps, at least, then she might be more likely to have the physical strength to either sort the tailgate or the pony, or better still both. Rubbish! No, she just needed to gain more experience and thereby knowledge.

"Here you go," she said, offering him a mug of steaming coffee.

"Oh, I don't take milk," he informed her, noting the colour.

Great, so she was back to being treated like a sub-human was she - master and servant? The ingratitude. No, stop it. She could be so childish at the most inappropriate of times. Sometimes so sure about herself, other times so submissive and timid, anyone with an ounce of arrogance in them could easily take advantage and walk all over her. It was an avoidable state of affairs. Often she could sense the confidence in her waning. Normally this would be triggered by the sour mood that would be escalating in the personality of the company she was keeping. So, all in all, she couldn't be to blame. It puzzled her. When these atmospheres eventually cleared, although never completely, did the instigator feel any guilt, or was it all purely her problem? This time she decided to intervene in an attempt to avoid the catalyst taking its toll.

"I can get you another one, no worries," she mimicked Tom.

"Do you mind?" he asked, more calmly and appreciative this time.

"Before you go, can you pass me that ointment and those bandages there please?" he asked, an arm raised up. A relaxed hand gestured in the direction of a holdall by the trailer.

She did better than that. Wanting to get back into his good books, and who knows maybe more when the day's work was over, she placed the bag beside him and gathered up the lead rein herself.

"Are you okay with that?" he said with concern. They both knew how flighty these ponies could be in normal circumstances. She knew he wasn't being wholly patronising.

"Yep," she replied, her heart pounding. He opened up a tub of liniment and applied it to the damaged area. The pony limped about between them.

"Shh, alright girl. I know it's cold," he sympathised with the animal.

When he had finished bandaging the injured limb he got up from the ground and took the pony away from the trailer, before it did any more harm to itself. He was looking down at the pony's legs as it struggled with the pain.

"That smarts, doesn't it?" he acknowledged, patting the animal's neck.

"Right, where's that number?"

They both went into the house, heading into separate rooms. She to the kitchen, he to contact Tom and persuade him to come over with his own trailer.

He explained the situation through apologies for disturbing Tom's break. Tom was surprisingly good about it, promising to get there as soon as he'd finished helping Scott and Ben with their sheep.

True to his word, Tom pitched up steering his trailer around the top of the drive and around the tight left bend that took him into the yard, up against the kitchen. He turned off the engine, jumped down out of the cabin and slammed the driver's door behind him. Recognising the trailer and the sound of his voice, she felt her body tense. He would be sure to figure out what they had been up to. Betrayal. That's what it was. Traitor. Having let him see how deep her feelings ran for him at his own farmstead, it hadn't taken her long to fill that dreadful hole he had torn into her. But that wasn't it. Tom was an arrogant challenge to her sensitive female emotions. The other times it was lust and the ferocious battle she would put herself forward for with a good looking, horny man. That wasn't entirely accurate either. Self-esteem still intact, she convinced herself. She could be choosy, fussy even. So, if she was so selective, why, why, why did she seem to constantly discover the bullish ones? The real problem was that she read into things too much. In truth, she was neurotic, melodramatic too. For now she was exhausted, wanting only to lay down there and then where she stood beside the kettle. She held one hand on the handle, trying to muster the energy to pour a cup for each of them. The yoghurt caught her eye again. She left the drinks and helped herself to some more of that deliciously sweet, comforting, pink concoction. It was warm now. She couldn't decide whether she was enjoying it or not. Her vivid imagination managed to conjure up an image of a pile of splattered vomit. Staring into the plastic pot in her hand, she began to feel a little like being sick herself. Water. A sensible person would be downing water like there was no tomorrow. Maybe for her there wouldn't be a tomorrow the way her head was pounding. There she went again, being dramatic and self-pitying. She poured a pint glass for herself and almost finished drinking it before Tom came in. He stood in the doorway, flicking his cigarette ash into a half-empty, half-full can of something, or tin as they were known to be called out here. It made her think of parties she had been to where she had agreed to partake of a beer. If only merely to keep up the alcohol level in her system when the wine had been exhausted. As drunk as she was, she would never allow herself to get so hammered that she didn't remember to shake the can and listen for cigarette ends. Still, she wouldn't be staying there tonight if all went to plan. That was if the ponies and the trailer could be taken care of.

"Have you got a coffee for me there then?" Tom asked her. She blushed, partly at seeing him, partly by the very fact that he was addressing her and a little to do with her obvious laziness. What a slob. Stood in her yoghurt-stained clothes, gorging herself on food that she hadn't even bought. So, she was a thief as well. God, she was a mess. Why did he have to see her like that? She made the drinks, while he seemed to stare at her all the while.

"There," she said, bluntly and passed him two cups, one with milk, one without, handles pointing towards him. Of course she remembered how Tom took his coffee, like she hadn't forgotten the words he had whispered to her when things were smoother between them.

"Cheers," he replied, taking a grip of the coffees, his cigarette placed back in his pouting, gorgeous mouth. Why was he so kissable? He was such a pig, but an irresistible one with it.

"Do you want a hand?" she called after him.

"No, you're alright, we'll sort it," he returned.

She made up her mind to let them get on with their men's work and took a slurp of coffee. Knowing it would dehydrate her further, but past caring. She went into the bathroom, placing the cup on top of the cistern, and looked at her face in the mirror, scrutinisingly. What a sight! Her mascara was all smudged below her lower lid. Patches of dry skin had left her cheeks with cracks and flaky areas, which she could see the sun was catching, irritatingly. She thought about the light sheering through the window, beside the kitchen sink, where she had been standing, talking to Tom.

"Oh, brilliant," she said to the mirror. "You look awful," she announced.

Next to the cold tap was a pot of Vaseline. She wiped some of it into her face in the vain hope it might relive the disfigurement. Instead it just sat there and she had to resort to using the dank bath mat to wipe the grease away, given there wasn't a towel in sight. She scanned the remainder of the room, spotting a pot of men's designer moisturiser. It smelt of cheap Christmas presents she had bought her brother as a young teenager, but out of necessity she applied it anyway, smoothing it into the traces of make-up in circles around her eyes. There was an awful second when she panicked she had got some of the cream in her eye, closing it automatically. Reaching blindly out for the cold tap in preparation to rinse the eye out, she blinked repetitively and paced up and down on the spot with the stinging. Fortunately the discomfort subsided. She left the tap alone and opted for a piece of tissue that she folded over and this time carefully cleaned away the affected area.

"That's better," she declared and with that she took a sip of her coffee and followed it with a capful of mouthwash, which again didn't belong to her. It was the season of goodwill after all!

She took another tentative sip of her coffee, grimaced and tipped the rest of it into the basin. Not wanting to turn into another slob like the rest of the household appeared to be, she returned the empty cup to the kitchen, there to find her two ever so dishy male companions hard at it at the table, with their steaming coffees. One had his chair tilted back on its legs towards the sink, so that she couldn't come by, either to place her cup down for washing or to get to her room. The other, Tom, had one arm placed on the table, where his mug was, the other arm was bent and propped over the back of his chair, a smoking cigarette teetering between his fingers. The room was choking her a little and she noticed in the ashtray, between the men, at least another three cigarette butts they must have consumed between them already. It was times like these that she remembered why smoking was so anti-social, yet still they almost made the men seem harder for it. No doubt she was biased considering she fancied the pair of them. God, let's face it, she just fancied men, full stop. Nothing wrong with that, she was young, relatively fit, even if she did say so herself, fairly attractive too when she made an effort, a big effort. The issue was really hormones, theirs and hers. From what she had seen of them, they weren't short of a few of them. Theirs were raging.

She was trying to think of something interesting, smart, clever even, to tell them but nothing came. Instead, Tom pushed his chair back and hauled himself up.

"Right, I'd better get them off then," he said.

"Are you okay with everything else?" he asked cryptically.

"Sure. Yep, thanks mate. I'm going to be getting off as well Tom, so enjoy. I owe you one."

Sudden panic inside of her made her feel quite light-headed and almost nauseous again. She wasn't mentioned at all. When she considered the history they had between the three of them, plus the fact that she was under the impression she was meant to be coming on this trip up the east coast today. Not to mention it was Christmas, well, the day after anyway. Say something, say something, she thought to herself. God, why was she so incapable of telling them what was on her mind? Why was she so inept, so anxious, so absolutely terrified to make a mistake? What did she have to lose?

"Erm, excuse me guys," she started. Why did she use that word, guys?

"What?" they replied. Their faces still turned away from hers.

Tom had been a shit towards her for what seemed like forever now, so no change there, but now it was like boys together stuff, games they get a kick out of playing, or something. Maybe she made them feel intimidated, as if. She decided to alter her tone somewhat.

"Are you sure I can't do anything to help?" she asked them, turning her head to face them both, desperately trying to make her smile to them appear as genuine as possible. She could have a cheeky glint in her when the mood took her. It was a kind of involuntary thing, but she still tried to bring it on where possible. This was one of those moments. The two men turned to look at her and she knew she had got halfway in succeeding to reduce their surly mood.

"No, have a good Christmas. Well, what's left of it," answered Tom. Then, as he moved towards the kitchen door he placed a warm hand on her backside, then left. To top it all, she got the same again with the parting of his sidekick. She grinned alone, stood for a minute relishing in everything that had happened to her, before going outside herself. She spotted some rugs that needed to come in off the washing line and made her way across the garden to reach them, positioning herself so she could watch as Tom left. He was taking the ponies on his trailer to his own farmstead. The whole scene made her remember times spent with him, just the two of them, well them and the bull under the tree, the cows, sheep, her garden where she had toiled for hours on end. She heard a sigh and let her eyes wander up and away with the dust trail of Tom's truck as it sped off in a southerly direction. But just as she was really beginning to feel a whole lot better she noted Tom take a right-hand turn at the fork in the road. He, the trailer, the ponies, were all heading off to Pagets. Now what would he be wanting to go there for, she pondered sarcastically to herself. As if she had forgotten which of his favourite grooms lived there, at least of those who were currently based in Tamauri. She felt deflated and the hangover was kicking in again. Maybe it was all in her mind? Tom certainly was anyway.

Taking the rugs into the house, she caught sight of her other bed fellow pouring some petrol into the car they were now supposed to be taking for their excursion. Feelings of guilt manifested themselves as she hadn't offered any kind of contribution by way of cash or anything else equally practical to help with the journey. Where they were meant to be staying each night hadn't featured in her mind either, nor the expense of that. A sickly panic rose up in her. Christ, she could be so naïve, thoughtless, foolish even sometimes. It wasn't as though she had assumed she wouldn't need to pay for anything much. She simply hadn't given the Christmas break much thought. It was always work, work, work with Tom and on the farm. Whenever she could grab the opportunity to relax, which was often with Tom's high-spirited sister, she would find herself drunk before she could say "let's be sensible and put some extra money aside for that trip up the east coast." Too late now. Still, she did have some spending money from Tom's meagre salary he paid her. Perhaps she could stretch that out and cut back on the drinking? Chance would be a fine thing, gathered the company she was keeping.

"Can you lock up?" he asked of her, tossing her the keys to the house.

"Okay," she answered, relieved at having caught them, rather spectacularly she thought.

"Are we all set?" she asked him, still slightly embarrassed and proving so by the blush on her cheeks. She turned so her face wasn't so noticeable to him.

"Think so. Get a move on then," he told her impatiently.

"Yes, yes, yes. Coming," she retorted, skipping over some empty bottles parked up in a crate and just in her pathway.

"Climb in," he told her. She hauled herself into the car, carefully positioning her feet either side of a bag that he had thrown in the footwell in front of her seat. She noticed there was also a tattered map, together with a bottle of water and his wallet. Well, at least he had come prepared. He spotted her looking at it and winked.

"Help yourself," he offered. "But give me a sip first," he added afterwards.

She blushed again. No, of course he didn't mean his money. She wasn't a prostitute or anything was she?

"Oh look, can you just check inside my wallet to see if I have my driver's licence in there?" he asked her. She popped open the button releasing the contents over her lap as she did so.

"Sorry," she offered.

"Don't worry. It's full of junk," he informed her, starting up the temperamental engine for the third time.

"Oh come on, darling," he told the car out loud. It started simultaneously.

Casting an eye over his personal effects she spied a passport photograph of a young brunette woman. She was attractive looking, though she seemed terribly out of place amongst the random receipts and the odd lining of a cigarette packet.

"Your sister?" she enquired nosily.

"Girlfriend," he replied in a matter-of-fact way.

"Oh!" was all she could muster. She tried to make it sound like a question, more than an accusation.

"We don't see much of each other," he explained.

It wasn't explanation enough for her, not to excuse the events of last night with her. Thankfully, she found his licence, poking its head above the partitions that held his notes.

"Here it is," she announced, handing him what he'd asked for.

"No, keep it in there," he asked her. It gave her another opportunity to look over his girlfriend's picture. She had brown eyes. She was jealous of her already, believing anyone with brown eyes would never seem to look old, even when they supposedly were. The normally unflattering passport photo showed the girlfriend in a good light, in her judgement. Her complexion was fair, clear more importantly and there was continuity in the great looking condition of the curls that seemed to bounce just above her shoulders. Her mouth was held in a pose as if she had been laughing about something funny he was telling her at the time - secrets between the two of them. Three's a crowd, she thought to herself.

"She's pretty," she told him, as if he had never thought so himself.

"She's alright," he said.

It was as though he didn't want to reveal too much about the woman, nor his relationship or feelings for her. He could be such a private man when he wanted to be, but with a few drinks inside him such an entertainer, sharing everything of himself to anyone who cared to be in his company.

"Oh come on, she's gorgeous," she informed him, sounding a touch over the top in her compliment to the stranger staring back at her, the lips and teeth in silent laughter.

"Fancy her, do you?" he laughed at her.

She had gone too far. He must think she was jealous. She was. He gave her knee a gentle squeeze, sliding his hand up her thigh. The action turned her thoughts away from the picture and she looked at him in wonderment. He winked, saving her insecurities and shame. As they came to the junction he removed his hand from her leg again and took full control of the car, taking them left, north and onwards on their journey.

They had been travelling for a number of hours before she realised she hadn't offered to give him a break from the driving at all. She was getting herself worked up, trying to pluck up the courage to be as good as her word, if she offered at all. Again he had come more prepared than her with his international licence. She hadn't brought one at all.

"Are you alright?" she asked him for the umpteenth time that day, meaning wasn't it about time they took a pit stop. Was he certain, after all that alcohol last night and the definite lack of sleep, that he could still guarantee he wouldn't fall asleep at the wheel?

"Actually, I'm going to find somewhere for us to get some rest," he told her, opening the window on his side to let out his cigarette smoke.

"Good," she said, eternally grateful.

Another hour passed, this one with her head nodding constantly as she tried desperately to keep herself from falling asleep. It was the least she could do to keep him company and make gratifying gestures at the beautiful scenery about them as they thundered along the roads.

THE HOTEL

"Right, this will do," he said sleepily, applying the handbrake as they parked up in the hotel car park.

"God, are you sure?" she said, shocked by the fact they appeared to be about to enter an immensely smart hotel - knowing full well the small amount of savings she had brought would in no way cover the cost of a meal there, let alone a room or rooms for the night. She wished he was a better communicator and had put her in the picture. In her experience, men were rarely good communicators. Now was the time to come clean with him.

"I'm sorry, but I haven't got enough on me to afford this," she explained, telling him as if there was more money at home or in England that she could access if needs be. A complete exaggeration of the truth she knew, but he had placed her in a very embarrassing position, a forte of his it seemed.

"That's alright, my treat," he said. Total relief. She relaxed and smiled at him as though to say I hope this smile is sufficient for now, to let you know how grateful I am and that I think you're the most generous, kindest, the best. How excited was she, like a child.

It was after midnight. She was amazed and impressed to see the Reception was still manned at that hour.

"It's in the name of Jones," he told the immaculately dressed man who stood between the hotel room keys and the reception desk.

"Right sir. Yes I see." The man glanced down at the computer screen and punched a few buttons.

"Here we are, sir. Up the stairs, left, along the corridor and yours is the second on the right after the fire hydrant, sir," he explained and handed over a plastic card that she realised was to unlock and lock their room door.

"Thank you, and that's for you," handing over something which she assumed must have been a tip.

Oh! my God, he had booked in advance. Planned the whole thing, she worked out as she followed his heels up the stairs. Suddenly, it was rather sobering. She felt slightly deflated, annoyed at his presumption. But then she couldn't afford this by herself and besides she could be in for more fun yet to come if she was right that he had only paid for one room. She ought not to assume too much herself though. Most likely it was a twin and after all that driving he was probably going to crash out.

When they reached the room the first thing he did was to switch on the television and scan through to the sports channel. Please don't be predictable. He reached with a hand to the mini-bar, whilst perched at the front of one of the beds and pulled out two miniature gins and a tonic water. She pre-empted his request and handed him one of the glass tumblers she had spied in the ensuite.

"Here, I think it's meant for our toothbrushes," she said to him.

"Cheers. Help yourself."

She did, even though she wasn't really in the mood. There was a quarter bottle of a local chardonnay she recognised from one of the polo grounds she had worked at. It slipped down beautifully. Sauntering over to the curtains she pulled one side back a little and stood ogling at a man and woman, on the opposite side to an illuminated courtyard, who looked like they were arguing about something. She couldn't understand how anyone could pick a time and a place like this to start rowing. Taking her eye downwards she watched the silent fountain rise and splash down to the yellow water below. The bottom and sides of the water feature were tiled with a mosaic pattern that she recognised as the same emblem on the main doors of the hotel. A movement from one of the couple regained her attention. She looked up and across again. They were making up now, kissing each other. He was running his hand through her hair and holding her face, sliding his fingers down to her neck and shoulder, pushing the dress she wore over her shoulder and down her arm, then the other side. It made her feel warm down below, moist even. She was getting excited again.

Remembering she had company of her own, and not wanting to be accused of being some sort of peeping Tom or voyeur, she let the curtain fall back. Then she turned her attentions to her roommate. Clearly, he could read her mind. Far from being transfixed to the sport he had turned the box off now and had located the hotel music system. A popular band was playing a tune she recognised that made her feel good inside, carefree.

He placed his drink beside the television and threw himself backwards onto the bed. Right, he was for it now. How else was she going to show him her appreciation? She came and stood in front of him, hands on hips, leant forwards from the waist and began to undo his belt, sliding the strap through the buckle with a slap. It amused her. His eyes were closed but at the noise he opened one ajar and grinned.

"What are you up to, trouble?" he asked her.

She was feeling wicked now and sticky too.

"Be quiet you," she commanded him, teasingly tugging at his chinos, pulling them with an effort over his hips and down his thighs to the hotel carpeted floor. The buckle made a chink as it made contact with the ground.

"Are you enjoying yourself down there?" he asked of her.

"Not as much as you will be in a minute," she let him know.

He laughed and raised his legs up to dislodge the ends of his trousers from his feet, pushing off his Docksiders from the heel. She had noticed he had a tan line on his feet from not having worn any socks for a while and now she could see the whiteness of his toes, brilliant in the darkness of the room. He was grasping her outer thighs now. Then, with a heave-ho, she was hoisted up and onto him.

"I've got a little present for you," he told her gleefully.

She had totally forgotten he had gone to the trouble to buy her a Christmas present.

"Oh, you shouldn't be so modest" she joked,, still embarrassed at the thought she wasn't going to be in a position to reciprocate.

He giggled, childishly. It was quite attractive to her that he could let that hard guard down sometimes. He struggled to reach a hand down to his trousers and seeing the effort he was having to make she passed them up to him, twisting her back and almost doing herself a mischief in the process.

"Careful now," he said, smirking. "You're not as young as you think," he added. His turn to tease.

"Thanks," he said. Inside one of the back pockets was a small flat package. It was gift-wrapped with a red foil bow that had become crumpled in transit.

"Can I open it?" she asked.

"Well it is a Christmas present after all," he replied.

She was blushing again. How ridiculous to ask such a question. Hurriedly, in the hope she would forget her blushes and make a speedy recovery, she slid the bow off from the paper beneath, then tore off the Sellotape to reveal another box beneath. It too had a covering.

"What's this? Pass the parcel?" she wondered.

"Get on with it." He sounded half annoyed, half excited.

It was a photo frame. She knew it was the wrong size to be of any type of small and potentially exorbitantly expensive piece of jewellery, say such as a ring or more likely a pair of earrings. Then she had imagined or willed it to be a bracelet with a matching necklace. Not that she was horribly religious, but a crucifix would have been appreciated, gold perhaps? She felt greedy, not very attractive at all if she wanted to gain his respect. Whatever, it was going to be, she was going to look thrilled. That was exactly what she wanted. But a photo frame? It was a surprise all right. She was beginning to confuse him with her grandmother, in his choice of gifts. And who in the world was he getting her mixed up with?"

"A photo frame," she announced trying to raise the flattened level and tone of her voice. The sound came out like a cat meowing.

"Yep. Thoughtful of me, wasn't it? he stated. "It's silver-plated," he pointed out.

"Really. You shouldn't have," she told him, truthfully.

"You hate it, don't you? Not that I give a shit," he laughed.

"Oh look, I haven't bought you anything. How can I make it up to you, I wonder?" she humoured him.

Placing the present behind her on the television cabinet, she turned back to him. His hands were brushing her outer arms. There was a slightly embarrassing silence in the air.

"So, what did you get your girlfriend?" she asked him. Pause. Awkwardness. Tension. Regret.

"Why are you asking? Not jealous are we?" he responded.

"No." She knew immediately she had said it too quickly. She was embarrassed now. Why did she ask? She didn't really want to know. After all, she would only be comparing presents and working out how much they both meant to him, accordingly. Yep, she was jealous all right. What a crippling state of affairs. Jealousy. It was one of those emotions that tended to be chronic if it got a hold of you. Women seemed to be more prone to it. What an ugly feeling to hold and behold, particularly of the fairer sex. It almost sounded like a delicacy, a sweetie, a pudding, like jelly. All that this conversation was achieving was leaving a nasty, bitter taste in his mouth.

He stood up, almost knocking her on the head and sending her flying, but she was half prepared. Her head was bent down in regret. Damn, damn, damn. Single-handedly she had managed to spoil a potentially beautiful relationship. Stay positive. All was not lost. Let's think this through. He had a girlfriend. That much was true. Someone he was pretty serious about as well because he carried her photograph. God, what a mess. It was almost like a threesome with the third person, namely his girlfriend back home, unaware in England, being incognito. Feelings of guilt and shame enveloped her. Poor lass, trusting her man implicitly to leave her side and travel the world, safe in the knowledge that he would return to her once more. Well, it was certainly true he was planning on going back eventually. Actually, it was quite likely to be soon after the Christmas break, by the sounds of things.

"Look, I'm sorry," she announced.

"Sorry for what?" he tormented her.

"Sorry I asked. Sorry you have a girlfriend and sorry you cheated on her."

"We," he added. "Let's have some clarity here. It takes two. You were a willing party in this, so don't lay all the blame on me. Anyway, what she doesn't know won't hurt her."

"That's not the point."

"What is the point, exactly?" he asked. Right now things were getting very chilly in here.

"The point? The point? The point is ... It's Christmas and we still have some celebrating to do."

"No, no, no. You don't get off that easily." He seemed serious. She felt quite anxious now. No one knew they were staying there. He could do anything to her if he wanted to. It was frightening, almost. Now things could go very easily either way. He seemed temperamental that way, depending on what he had been drinking usually. She thought to herself. Champagne again. He was all right with that before. They were at opposite ends of the room now, he lighting a cigarette for himself and peeping, side on, at the suite opposite theirs, she perched on one of the twin beds. Flicking through the channels she caught some news from home, their home.

"Come and see this," he said to her, flicking the cigarette embers into a hotel ashtray behind him. "There's a hell of a lot of passion going on over there and neither of them can be a day under sixty. Must be Viagra!" he declared informatively.

"That's not old. Look, there's been trouble at home. The weather has been terrible, people getting snowed in and everything." It was a distraction both of them were relieved by.

"Yes, but we're nice and snug in here, gorgeous, aren't we, you little minx." He told her, squeezing next to her on the edge of the bed.

"Budge up then, fatty," he nagged.

Why did men do that, or the ones she came to know? Throw you the best compliments; call you 'gorgeous', which though slightly over-doing things was very welcoming to the ear, only to take it all back with a one-liner like that. And they say we play games? It was as if they got some kick out of toying with our emotions. Good job their tackle was as sensitive to touch, or there would be precious little alternative to getting through to them as effectively.

"Me fat?" she declared, knowing it to be untrue, though she was starting to develop a complex, momentarily, anyway.

She thought about putting him down but could appreciate his humour. There was no need to be offensive. They were patching things up between them now, best not to ruin things. Life was better being his friend than not, or easier.

"Really, you shouldn't be missing these two going for it," he repeated.

"Jealous are we?" she retorted, playing him at his own game. "Maybe you'd like a game of swingers? Like a bit of couple-swapping do we? Fancy a bit of old muff?" she asked.

"Oh, stop it. For a nice girl with your background you can be really very crude at times. Honestly, it's terribly unbecoming," he announced.

"It's terribly unbecoming," she teased.

With that he grabbed her about the waist as she neared him and pushed her up against the glass. Her breasts were bulging out of the sides of her bra with the pressure on them. The window was cold and it took her breath away for a second. Her nipples started to become erect with the change in temperature and from being next to his naked body. She forgot she was almost naked too and thought of the man and the woman across from them and what they must think. What did it matter though? They would be out of there by morning and need never go to the trouble of making their excuses. Also, this couple were being exhibitionists themselves, so what was wrong with it?

When she looked though, the opposite apartment was dark.

"They've worn themselves out. Look, their lights are out now. They must have gone to bed. Maybe the drugs have worn off?" she said.

"Oh, no they haven't," he said with excitement. "Look, look, look, look," he said hurriedly. "There, on the floor. My God, do they ever stop?"

"You can talk," she told him and with that she thrust a hand up and between his legs and held him there.

"Come on then, you. We can't be beaten by the old-timers over there. Let's show them how it's done," he giggled, grabbing her warm hand and unleashing himself from her clutches.

They made their way back over to the bed.

"No wait. I've got a better idea," he declared, then led her by the scruff of her hair towards the shower cubicle in their hotel room.

By now she was feeling fairly wasted. It was almost dawn now and she was starting to sober up and dwell upon the fact they were meant to be continuing their excursions today, which meant more quality time in that stinking car. When all at once he threw the cold tap on full blast and pushed her bodily against the ice-cold tiles under the water. The hard jets from the shower head pulsed down onto her now bare breasts and her tummy. Screaming with the sensation, he had to muffle the noise and reluctantly bring on the heat a touch, only enough to take the chill off.

"Hush," he ordered, grabbing the bar of soap from its gold-plated dish beside him. He lathered them both all over, creating soapy bubbles up the walls and on the base where they stood. She reached for the complimentary shampoo and succeeded in unscrewing the top, depositing a dollop onto her locks. In circular movements she removed any trace of him in her hair, then started to wash his. He allowed her, closing his eyes as she massaged his scalp, moving down to his neck and shoulders. He moaned with approval. He was taut.

Then, in a flash, she was lying in a crumpled heap at his feet, pulling him down to her.

"What are you doing down there?" he asked her.

"I slipped on the soap," she said between giggles.

"You mean this soap?" he laughed squeezing the slippery bar up through his hand, smoothing it in between her inner thighs and letting it splosh into the frothy water about them. They were both feeling childish now, joking through laughter and tears. He collapsed out of the shower and onto the carpet near the mini-bar. Opening the door he picked out a vodka and tonic mixture.

"Here. This might help to pick you up," he joked, rolling the bottle to her.

"Cheers," she called out from the noise of the cascading water. "Could you pour it for me, though?" she asked him, standing up now and rinsing out the remains of the shampoo.

"Isn't it a bit early for spirits?" she wondered.

"Not when it's Christmas, mate" he replied, mysteriously.

CHECKOUT

They must have got some sleep because there was definitely a void in their time together that neither could account for. When they came to, it was to discover they had been the victims to one or more unwanted guests.

"It's not here. It's not anywhere. I can't find it," he yelled.

"Find what?" she asked in a quizzical voice.

"My damn wallet, that's what," he replied. She suddenly had an image of the trouble they could be in if they didn't have any money or credit to pay their hotel bill. She wished she had been more organised in funding her own trip and less presumptuous, less reliant on him. The next thing that occurred to her was that her purse, or wallet - call it what you will - might be missing too? Thankfully there were no credit cards or driving licence in hers, and only a little cash. Driving licence? Oh fantastic! They were going to be stuck, penniless with no wheels either. Still, she could think of worse places. She started to help him look, though secretly she was concerned about how they were going to pay their bill and enjoy the rest of their trip, more than whether or not some low-life was making off with his credit cards, forging his signature and helping themselves to his fortune.

"Found it?" he asked her.

"No, you?" she responded.

"What do you think?" he snapped at her.

"Don't take it out on me. It wasn't my idea to carry on drinking into the early hours, until we were so off our faces we wouldn't have known if the bloody hotel had burnt to the ground!"

"Oh! now I think you're being a tad dramatic, and don't blame me for the amount of alcohol you were very happy to consume. After all, it's Christmas!"

She thought to point out to him that strictly speaking it wasn't Christmas any more, but there was a terrible atmosphere between them already.

"Have those thieving bastards taken your money as well?"

"I think so. I haven't seen my purse either. Luckily there wasn't much in there anyway."

"Lucky for who? Look, I'm going to go downstairs and complain about the piss-poor state of security they have in place here. Wait there."

"No, I'm coming down with you."

"No, I'll do the bollocking. Make yourself useful and pack up our gear."

"We can do that later. I'm coming with you and hearing for myself what kind of an explanation they've got for this."

"Excuse, more like. All right. Just grab my smokes will you? At least they have had the decency to leave me those."

"Maybe they weren't their brand?"

He smirked slightly and locked their room behind them, catching up with her along the hotel landing towards the lift.

"What's the matter? Have I sapped all the energy out of you that you can't face the stairs?"

"Oh, ha, ha. I wasn't even thinking."

"Well, why change the habit of a lifetime?"

They got in the lift along with a Chinese couple and fell into a stony silence. She felt her stomach rise and fall with a jerk and struggled with the acid build up inside of her.

"Right, here we are."

"Now, don't go in guns blazing. It's usually much more effective to be polite to people. You're more likely to get what you want that way, trust me."

"Fine, we'll try it your way first. Okay?"

They made their way over to the Reception desk and waited behind an elderly gentleman who appeared to be rather on the large size. Too many gourmet meals and fine wines in fancy hotels, maybe? The man finished his business, gathered his personal effects and moved aside.

"Good morning, sir, madam."

"Good morning. Well, actually it hasn't been a good morning for us. It seems as if we have been robbed."

"Robbed, sir?"

"Robbed, you know. Taken advantage of; had our possessions pinched, stolen, burgled."

"Oh, I see, sir."

"Well, we were wondering what you were going to do about it?"

"Me, sir?"

"Yes, you sir."

"Well, I'll just fetch the Manager for you, sir."

"Jolly good."

"Right away, sir."

The man at the Reception rang a bell on the counter in front of him and lifted a phone to his ear, tapping in an extension number in the process. He raised an eye and made an attempt at a reassuring, everything in control, type of smile.

A young lad came over and stood to attention behind them, heels together, waiting patiently for his orders. The man who had called for him raised a finger as if to say, hold on a minute, muttering something between cheesy smiles down the line.

"Good, thank you for your help, sir." He came off the phone and spoke to the boy.

"Fetch these fine people a drink will you? What would you care for, madam? I believe there is fresh coffee, juice, tea - Earl Grey, English Breakfast."

She interrupted his seemingly endless list of a variety of teas.

"Earl Grey would be marvellous."

"And for you, sir? Complimentary of course."

What a nerve, he thought to himself.

"Coffee would be fine. Espresso."

"Good, sir. Right away, sir" he repeated, ushering the boy to get a move on with their request.

They positioned themselves in comfortable-looking leather armchairs in the lobby, where the Reception was still visible. Their beverages arrived at the same time as a tall, well-groomed gentleman in a very smart suit and immaculately polished shoes.

His dyed black hair was swept back, vampire style. He looked splendid, she thought.

"Sir, madam. Do you mind if I join you?"

"Sure."

"I gather you have had the misfortune of having a disturbance in the night."

"Well, in the early hours of the morning to be more exact."

"Right. Now what could you tell me happened? What has been taken precisely?"

"A good deal of money, that's what. Credit cards, driving licence, oh and my wife's Cartier watch. Is that precise enough for you?"

"I am sorry, sir. Please accept my sincerest apologies on behalf of myself and the staff here."

"Apology accepted. I just hope there haven't been any other bad luck stories here, like ours."

"Let me assure you, sir, this kind of thing has never happened before. At least not during my working life here."

"Well, I guess there's a first time for everything." He glanced sideways at his female companion and placed a hand down between them to squeeze her knee.

"What do we do now?"

"I think the matter should be reported to the police, sir, if you are in agreement? I could contact them on your behalf, if you prefer, sir?"

"No, no. Don't trouble yourself. I'll contact the credit card companies and dig out my insurance document. Although short of selling you my ravishing wife over here, I couldn't possibly tell you how I'm going to go about paying your bill."

"Leave that with me, sir. As far as I am concerned you have reacted to all this unpleasantness with the politeness and decorum of a true English gentleman."

She smiled, wondering whether the kindly Manager would have thought quite the same of this lad next to her if he had been able to see him in action last night. What a beast!

The Manager raised himself from the luxurious chair, making use of the armrests to hoist himself upright. He proffered a hand and the men shook on a gentlemen's promise. The one to cancel the debt of the other, whilst the underlying promise to the hotelier was not to run off to some newspaper to sell their story about the cheatings that were going on in their country's leading hotel chain.

"Tea?" he asked lifting the pot and circling it a touch to brew the leaves a little more.

"Perfect," she said, watching the now crumpled trouser legs of the Manager as he made his way back across the lobby to the Reception once more.

"There's your tea. I'll be back in a minute."

"Where are you off to now?"

"I'm going to use their phone and make some complimentary calls to the UK to sort out this mess."

"Well you know and I know you can never actually speak to a real person, or at least not a person working in England! It will be some bod in a call-centre in Delhi or somewhere where the bonus boys don't have to pay their support too much, and that's an understatement. There is so much unfairness in the world. One person taking advantage of another's misfortune. It all amounts to luck if you ask me."

"How do you mean?"

She wasn't sure if she wanted to continue this one, her head was throbbing, lips dry, eyes sore. Did she really mean to start some deep and meaningful conversation in her condition? Shouldn't she have just kept to chitter-chatter about kittens, or how wonderful it was to see such an abundance of wildlife in Britain now that the government was paying out subsidies to farmers to keep a natural meadow on their land?

"Well, you know. You or I could just as easily have been born in Africa as England."

She thought about her time in Belindi for a moment.

"It doesn't mean you have to stay there though, certainly not with our relaxed immigration rules."

Christ he could be so ignorant at times.

"Do you think it's as easy as that. Do you? That anyone there can just pack up their belongings, hop on a plane and wing their merry way to blighty, where of course any diseases and ailments they have will be treated swiftly and effectively by our highly organised, well-funded, fully staffed, pride of the nation Health Service? Whereas the only pride our nation seems to hold now, incredibly, is in our over-paid football team, oh, and the Queen."

"Finished?"

"No, as a matter-of-fact I haven't."

"Well, I think you've said enough for one morning for this poor head of mine. Haven't you got a hangover?"

"Yes. Thank you for asking. Do you have anything we could take in our room?"

"I think there's something in my wash bag in the bathroom. Be an angel and run up stairs and get them, please."

"I'll go but I'm not taking the stairs. I feel quite breathless."

"That's the drink. You're all right. Once we've finished these we'll grab our kit and head off up the coast again. Any objection?"

"No. Sounds good to me. By the way, what was all that about a watch?"

He laughed.

P L A Y E R S

She had some quite good times in Tamauri town. In fact she had a spectacular time. The physio sessions were marvellous, so relaxing. It was quite an oddity. A private practice where the main man kept Dalmatian dogs about the treatment areas, health and safety aside, and llamas in his garden. She really felt as though she was being pampered and didn't really miss the ponies at all. Surprisingly, since she had dreamed of the lifestyle she had with them, at least some of them.

A lot of time was spent with Tom's sister. She was great fun. She worked hard as a dentist's assistant, though always seemed to have time for a drink and a laugh. They went riding together before, once or twice, to a brilliant little bar, out in the middle of nowhere, like most places here. They sold Moscow Mules there, with ice and there was a place out front where they could tether their ponies. She felt like a real cowgirl.

It wasn't until she was introduced to a fellow Brit that her recuperation really started progressing. Basically, he encouraged, teased, persuaded and forced her to get up the courage and climb back on board. He warned her she wouldn't have a job to go back to after the Christmas break and that was only halfway near to the end of her stay out there. So, she stayed with this character down at his place of work, got back in the saddle and moved on.

Life was definitely better after that. She was doing her job again, but this time she felt she had friends she could call on. The physiotherapy continued, but not so often and she managed to tie in the appointments with visits to Tom's sister. There she could relax after a morning's work or better still, at the end of the day and often she would crash on a spare bed or sofa.

The polo season progressed in earnest too and she started to realise just what Tom was expecting of her. Sometimes that wasn't enough. Especially when he was having a bad game. At one time he came charging off the field towards her. He didn't even appear to be slowing down. She thought she might call his bluff and stand her ground. Maybe he would respect her for that, but he had a face like thunder. Her own face must have been a bit pale by now. They were virtually on top of her, mixing up the parched soil in front of her. Stop! They would stop. Tom half-heartedly turned the pony side on, as though he was still playing the game. He certainly was playing some game with her now anyway. She was racking her brain, going through all his requests and demands. There wasn't a thing she could think of that she hadn't done. Everything was covered, sorted. The ponies were either resting, ready to go, or playing. Then she spotted them. Just at about the same moment that he was bellowing something at her. He rarely spoke civilly to her since she was catapulted off the grey. The stirrups. The stirrup straps. One had snapped in two and part of it was hanging down, like the way she was feeling now.

No. No. Not this time. She couldn't be blamed for this one. He could yell all he liked, but that wasn't going to make the slightest difference. It was weird. He was sitting up there on the pony, screaming at her, insults, abuse, but it wasn't having any impact on her. She began to realise quite what sort of a man Tom was. Could a game really mean so much to a human being, that it could make them behave in such a way to another? Or was it rather, that he was afraid of killing himself out there?

Glancing around to count the number of onlookers, she was relieved to spot Tom's sister. Smiling at her as usual. She raised her eyebrows, in the comfort zone of being just behind her brother's right shoulder. That put everything into perspective. Well, this episode anyway.

She thought about telling Tom that it wasn't her fault. Contemplated letting him know what she thought of his behaviour and of him, even where he could take his stirrup leathers and put them. But she wasn't going to stoop to his level. So she just let him get on with his ranting and eventually he turned his wrist inward and took the pony off back into the game.

Another groom had organised his tack for him and sorted out a spare strap to replace the broken one. The same groom who had struck up a relationship with Tom of late. She had heard these two had been on and off with each other for some time and had a long history.

The irony of it all though was that the girl who had really got Tom smitten was English. Apparently, she had worked as his groom before her time, and had lived in the same house and down at Tom's place, virtually as his wife. What she would have given to have had that with him. Not now though. No so much anyway.

Tom's latest girl seemed very competent to her. Not only in all things polo, but around the farms too. She seemed to be able to drive any form of machinery, turn her hand to anything the men could do, yet she managed to retain a femininity about her. She was tall, bronzed, blonde, curvaceous, strong in every way. She truly admired her. She wasn't the prettiest girl on the block, but good-natured, young and still naïve as far as men were concerned. This was obvious when a week after the most spectacular of shows of public affection from Tom at her twenty-first, he apparently then dumped her for some German polo player he had secretly dated on tour. Well, at least that was his side of the story. Credit, where credit is due, she kept her cool and got on with the never-ending list of tasks to do about the farms, and whilst the polo season was still in full swing.

Eventually, the tournaments came to a finale and players whose teams had been knocked out began to say their goodbyes and disappeared to get on with their usual day jobs - farming usually. It saddened her actually. She had made one or two friends at least. Luckily, there was a reunion in the form of the Polo Ball and as it turned out, she was about to find out what the red-necked men about her really thought of her.

That lamb had really proved its worth at least and at some stage she had huge amounts of fun shopping with Tom's sister for a dress and shoes. So much for Michael's opinion and the same went for his attitude.

When she arrived at the Ball, Michael was the first to catch her eye, or perhaps she had caught his? He looked utterly astonished at how she had scrubbed up. She hoped he was impressed, at least for her own gratification and if she was honest, her confidence. She grabbed a drink instead and took a deep breath, looking about her and taking it all in.

Finally, the hard work was done, for the time being and at least for tonight she could let her hair down and wear girls clothes, not her scruffy, farming boots and chaps to protect her from chaffing her inner thigh on the saddles. It had actually got so she didn't bother with those either. With the heat and the fact she hoped she might get a bit of colour on her legs for her efforts.

Looking about her and trying not to appear anything but relaxed in her surroundings, she spied Tom's sister. She was wearing the pink dress they had found in town together. It had been her first choice, but she had to admit it looked one hundred times better on her friend. She began to feel more herself. There was even a sideways smile, of sorts, from Tom, who cut a good figure in his jacket and tie. Scott was there too. In fact, pretty much every soul she had met seemed to have dug out their Sunday best.

Michael had a new girl on his arm. A stunning golden haired creature, who looked as good in her tiny dress, she had scraped on to her tanned body, as she did on horseback in a pair of shorts. She was brilliant at riding and clearly a favourite with the boys. Michael looked like he was the cat who had got the cream. With beer and cigarettes in one hand and Juliette in the other, he was sorted.

The music system was playing some tune she recognised from her first days in Tamauri and opened up the flood gates of her memories. Then, outside, strangely, she spotted a truck and some characters line-dancing. She had come across this kind of entertainment a fair bit since she arrived and had joined in when she was in the mood, and that was the mood she was in tonight. She was going to make the most of every opportunity, but first she was going to get that other drink.

Standing at the bar were a number of fellows she knew for one reason or another. Cousins of Tom, mates, farm workers, grooms and players alike, were all standing shoulder to shoulder. She couldn't really get near enough to be seen, let alone heard. Not until Michael grabbed her, thrust a beer in her hand and turned back to the bar. But not before whispering in her ear how he thought she looked alright.

He didn't really appear much again, in her company at least, for the best part of the night. Not until she found herself being dragged almost into a bar, nearby. Most of the lads were in there, Michael included, and quite a number of the girls she'd seen about on the farms and around the polo field. The music was loud. There was a great feel about the place. She started to smile, in a natural, relaxed way, the booze taking hold.

Michael took her arm, just as the tune was changing to some slushy nonsense. She held her breath. Looked about her to see where everyone was. What was he going to do? Was he really that incensed with her incompetence as an employee of Tom's or was it merely her presence there that he detested? He was looking right into her eyes now and low and behold he was pushing his gigantic torso towards her. He was all rock solid. A smile. This time from him to her. She looked nervous, waiting for the mood to change. His gorgeous girlfriend was nowhere to be seen. He must be off his head to risk losing that stunner.

Then she gathered her wits. Who was she kidding? It was simply the drink talking and making all his moves for him. She wasn't going to look a fool and in front of all his burly mates too, not to speak of his arrogant brother. When the song finished and he had stopped his fun with her, she would walk calmly away and join in with something or someone else, some line-dancing again perhaps? They must have looked pretty great together even so. She enjoyed the moment. There hadn't been a second in her time out there in Tamauri when she had given any consideration for Michael, and here he was dancing with her, cheek to ruddy cheek. What was his game? He was a good mover. She had no idea there was this smooth, romancing side to him. But then maybe that was what made the girls swoon for him despite his mood swings. He was unpredictable. Dynamite, that's what he was - a hot fuse. So she was going to have to be careful, really careful.

The music changed and with it the atmosphere, which suddenly became electric for a different reason. The song had provoked a strip from one of the boys, who with much encouragement and cheer was now standing on a small round table, parading his pectorals for all and sundry. He swung his white shirt about his head in a three-sixty and let it fly over the heads of the throng. There was much whistling, feet stamping and she noticed one or two characters drawing back hungrily on their cigarettes, holding the butt between thumb and index finger and hurriedly supervising its extinguishment before looking up again for the finish. And what a finish! This guy wasn't about to disappoint his audience. They were going to get what they had come for and no mistake. In an unprofessional way, which succeeded in achieving a huge call from the bar to quicken up the action, he fumbled with first his buttonhole, then his zipper. At last and greeted with the loudest appreciation for the night's frivolities so far, he cast his jeans into the frenzied crowd, dropped his pants to the table top beneath and stood there two hands on his buttocks, his head tossed back like a victorious matador.

The whole place had erupted by now and the entertainer responsible didn't even get the chance to climb down from his stage set before it was sent flying from under him. She watched as he was congratulated for his performance and then sniggered to herself as she watched the smile rapidly wiped off his face when his girlfriend appeared. The two of them had a very public, very fiery barny, making amends with an equally fiery and passionate kiss. She looked down for a minute, not wanting to ogle. She felt a little jealous - nothing shameful in that.

Not long after all these shenanigans, the same stage was set again. This time it was the matador's lover. She hadn't been a party to anything like this since a travelling companion persuaded her to visit a Thai strip club, en route to Tamauri. She couldn't believe the girl would go through with it. She was brave, stupid maybe? What point was she trying to make? Perhaps she wanted to get her boyfriend to notice her a bit more or maybe it was simply to wind him up as payback for his embarrassing behaviour earlier? She was sure the girl would only go so far as to take her bra off. That way she would expect to retain some dignity all round. It wasn't looking like it was going that way though. Sure enough she copied her lover, mimicking his every last move. Challenging him with her wry looks every now and then, as he stood there, left arm resting at the bar, right crushing itself about his pint, cigarette blazing by itself in his hand. The smoke was snaking upwards and stroking his face, taunting him. The men about him were nudging him with their elbows and muscular shoulders. She could see the annoyance building up in his eyes, the eyebrows knitting, menacingly. Now his lips were pushed together and she guessed behind them would lie clenched teeth. His jaw was jerking to the side of him and over his shoulder, the jeering hit fever pitch, just at the moment his girl's knickers were seen to be soaring overhead.

The next thing that happened was almost too ferocious to watch. The female exhibitionist was bundled naked off the table, stripped of all her clothes. Someone threw over a jacket that was promptly and unceremoniously thrown over her, haphazardly. She saw her being dragged off, kicking and screaming something nonsensical. Then she was back again, the jacket on correctly now and a button or two fastened to cover her ample breasts. It reached down to her upper thighs at least and with that and a sweep of her hand she took a random drink from the bar next to her. Finishing whatever was in the glass, she tilted it to one side, smashed it against the wooden panelling by her thigh there and headed like a steam locomotive towards some random fellow in the corner. Thankfully she was prevented from causing too much long-term damage, but the man in question was lucky to keep his sight.

A brawl proceeded, partly par for the course she was led to believe, and later she worked out for herself what all the fuss was really about. Supposedly, the girlfriend had won a bet with a mate of her boyfriend's. A wager, if you please, that she wouldn't do just as her man had in posing to everyone without a stitch of clothing on. The mate had refused to cough up and his come-uppance, a glassing. As if that wasn't enough, those few hangers on, bent on a fight whatever, found themselves out on the street. Here allegedly one of the unluckier ones ended up with a knife wound and had to be taken to the nearest hospital. Somehow, out here in the sticks as they were, she imagined he would have had quite a journey.

Once all the fuss had died down, some of the crowd that had gathered in the mayhem, began to disperse. One or two were looking at their watches and she had a sudden wake-up call of sorts. She had allowed the night to carry her away with it, with no thought for the consequences the next morning when she would have to be at those ponies again. No rest for the wicked and all that. The second thing which concerned her, although not quite as much as the image she held in her head of Tom's disapproving face at her shabby efforts to exercise his equine team, she had nowhere to stay for the night. In fact, she hadn't given the matter a single thought, until now realising the time was approaching almost two in the morning.

Just as she was about to subject herself to a night sleeping rough somewhere, or alternatively sobering up sufficiently to drive herself back a few hours later, Michael appeared. Or rather he seemed to creep up behind her. She wasn't certain if he passed a hand over her buttocks, but it was all so quick and the drink was really hitting her now. He motioned to her that she should follow him, and not knowing or being certain of his intentions, she nervously did his bidding.

There was a blur and the next thing she realised she was in some car and Michael was driving. Without making herself look too obvious, she glanced innocently over her right shoulder and then twisted her neck to check all areas of the back seats. They were alone.

With no street lights to show her the way they were travelling, she watched the stars and kidded herself they were on the right track homeward, back to her increasingly welcome single bed. It was literally pitch black around them, aside from the odd constellation and a passing truck, blazing its headlamps at them, momentarily. Only when she spotted the illuminated eyes of the sheep and ponies and recognised the difference in sound of the gravelled unmade track, did she relax. Safe in the relief they were back.

Not a word had been spoken between them. For her part she was finding things hard enough to keep awake and thereby offer Michael some form of company. There was also the thought that she could very easily annoy her driver by saying something irritating to him, oddly enough. Somehow that idea did not fill her with confidence for her enjoyment, let alone her safety especially in light of the fact Michael was probably more inebriated than her good self. Besides, Michael didn't speak either. His actions were enough.

There came a point when she could not hold on any longer and one way or another Michael sensed her urgency and pulled over. Trying to disguise her desperation, she climbed out of the car as gracefully as a timid girl, full of alcohol and fatigue, could.

It was dark still and as such she thought she didn't need to be too discreet as to where she positioned herself. How wrong could she be! In mid-stream, Michael was up behind her again, this time caressing the side of her neck and behind her ear. What was the matter with him? Talk about mixed messages and then what was he thinking? She was taking a pee for goodness sake! She thought to herself that some people get off on that sort of thing, but she couldn't bring herself to imagine she was allowing herself to be a part of something like that, something not so much as erotic as weird. Besides, Michael had been giving all the wrong signals, or at the most no signals at all, which kind of amounted to the same thing. Now he was groping at her breasts, or was that fondling? She wasn't paying much attention, since her hands were trying to reach for her knickers and wrench them up again in case Michael had ideas in that department. Horror of horrors, could Michael take things into his own hands? He had got her to trust him in a way, the drink, the dance, a lift home. Could he be purely and simply be prepping her to attack her sexually now? They were out in that blackness, his word against hers, she a virtual stranger to a country miles from her own.

In the end, having almost entirely sobered up, she thought the best thing to do would be to play it cool and make out he hadn't scared the living daylights out of her. She came to her senses, clothes still intact, but only just and softly, very softly, took his broad, warm hands and placed them down at his sides, whilst she slowly turned to face him. She gave him as friendly a smile as she could, in the circumstances. Incredibly, he smiled back, but with such feeling and tenderness, it uneased her still further. He moved aside as if to say, alright you're free. Though the smile had told her he wasn't going to leave it at that.

Just as soon as they were back at the house and before Michael had even time to switch off the ignition, she was inside. Planning how best she could re-hydrate herself, ready for a hard day's work, down at the yard in less than a few hours. She reached into a cupboard in the kitchen for a glass. In the corner of her eye she thought she caught the red and white check of Michael's shirt. She turned to see him disappear around a left-hand corner, which led to his bedroom. Her room was on the right. The thought of bed hurried her up a little and she filled the glass with water and finished it as quickly. There was a small part of her that was surprised, perhaps a tiny bit disappointed at Michael's decision to get his head down and not have it out with her, whatever it was he had started on the road out there. It must have been the drink again and so she went to go to her own bed.

Then all of a sudden someone else was in the kitchen with her, standing just where she needed to go. It was Scott. He smiled at her with a little more enthusiasm than usual, even for him. For once, she didn't feel comfortable with him. As far as she knew everyone in the household was back and most likely asleep, even Michael, given how tired and drunk he must have been. She tried to shake off her unease, but Scott looked as though he was after something, after her. What was this? There must have been some Greek mythology that she could make some analogy with now? Or was this more akin to something more modern, the father, the son and the polo groom? It might make great reading!

Scott had never been physical with her, certainly not tactile anyway. Sure, he had helped her find her way about the ponies, the yard, the farm and that sometimes required physical contact, that was unavoidable, acceptable. Now he was holding both of her hands, and given her position as a worker there, not to say the age difference, this didn't feel acceptable to her. Still, she had no intention of offending him and left her hands there in his for as long as she dared.

He was married for Christ's sake. Worst still, his wife was only along the corridor and had a habit of waiting up for him, even at this late hour. She could walk in on them any moment now. There would be trouble, big trouble. On top of every mishap she had been a party to. Nothing would compare with this. She thought about how good his wife had been to her, how she would break her heart, over something so innocent too. But it would have looked more than the two of them merely holding hands. Why would they feel the need to hold each other's hands, to be standing here like that, alone, at this hour, in the dark almost? Was he planning more with her? Was

Michael going to make a re-appearance and join in the fun and games?

She found herself virtually mesmerised at the hands. She could hardly stand straight for booze and fatigue. What was that expression, being drunk with fatigue? What was she now then, double drunk? A fool maybe, to keep standing there like that, gambling with her station within the house. She was running the risk of losing one good friend in Scott's daughter, if no one else, aside from potentially wrecking a marriage of nearly thirty years.

Scott stopped it in the end. Saved them both from the embarrassment, the shame, the disgust, the upset of it all. He cupped his hand under her chin and raised her face to his lips. He kissed her warmly. She felt he needed to show her she meant something to him, though possibly he didn't know quite what. The kiss was neither passionate, nor weak enough to be considered platonic.

Moving away from him as if they were playing a child's game, she walked slowly and in a backwards fashion in the direction of her bedroom. He stood there, half smiling, half a look of consternation. Their time was ended.

Diving under her covers, almost for protection, she allowed herself a mere second or two to reflect on the night's events, before falling asleep.

She believed she was sleeping and probably dreaming also when Michael whispered something in her ear. Well, she must have only just nodded off, because she heard him alright, smelt him too with those farm smells, the ponies, the cigarettes, drink. Oddly enough it didn't repulse her. He was manly through and through. She could certainly tell that now, with his hulk rubbing up against her back the way it was. Still too drowsy to tell what was truly happening she went to turn her head to face this intruder. The next thing Michael had pounced on top of her and now he was grappling with her shoulder to turn her on to her back and face him. She could very easily have lain there. He wasn't bad looking, far from it and God did she feel sex-starved. But that was it, wasn't it? She was desperate and he knew it. Moreover, considering how easy he seemed to find it to get his own way in the bedroom department, she seemed to be going to make this one a walk over. He was probing at her now with that smoking barrel of his. She was struggling to find it in her to resist him, that physique, the charm as he murmured this and that in her ear. The heat they generated made her draw in huge gulps of air and as she did so, part of her was knowingly teasing him, holding her mouth in that way.

This time though, she wasn't going to be the one rejected and left out in the cold. She pushed him off her with as much effort as if to say to him that she wasn't kidding. He didn't put up much of a fight anyway and once she had hissed a few times that he should go back to his own bed or someone might find them, he took the message and slithered away.

Really, he was probably thinking to himself already, that the whole thing was a bad idea, which he would regret enormously the following day. Besides, he had those paddocks to plough before sunset. They didn't talk much after that, but then they had never had a great deal to say to each other anyway. He had another girl on his arm within the week and their possible night together was history.

Entertainment did not comprise solely of brawls in the streets and pub fights out in Tamauri. Sometimes, she found herself with a drink in her hand enjoying a live band in some bar with Tom's sister. There was one night she could recall in particular when a fiddle player simply lit the room up with her gift in music. Being a visitor to the town, she was unfamiliar with the usual goings on, events and so forth. That evening she had been enjoying the company of her friends until they seemed to be making plans to head off to a regular haunt of theirs. They grabbed her under the arm in a friendly manner, the way mates do when they have all had fairly equal quantities of cheap local beer and wine, and off they all staggered.

The bar was a traditional old-fashioned place. It had a pool table, worn-out bar stools, rubbed away on the edges where the sitter had shifted his weight towards the bar, or the friend he was straining to hear telling him some joke or other. The same could be said for the roll-top wooden bar, polished and worn from forearms propping it up. Even the lights looked like they had seen better days, they matched the nicotine-stained ceiling above them and no doubt the shredded carpet under their feet. Still, it was an enormously homely place and in spite of Tom and Michael being present, she found she wasn't so bothered for once.

Everyone seemed to be really very relaxed, more than normal she thought. She couldn't put her finger on it, but it was one of those times when she wanted to capture that sense of contentment, of mass enjoyment and good companionship.

That was even before the band came on and started tuning up. She had played one or two instruments herself at school, though she got the feeling these musicians were quite special. They had a drum kit comprising the basics, the essential bass and acoustic guitars for country pub tunes. Though best and most interesting of all, a fiddler with an amplifier and she was on fire! The hype in the place crescendoed to such heights the girl with the fiddle took it upon herself to clamber up on the bar. Fiddle under chin, back bent over in rhythm to the music, up and down like some clockwork toy with one leg turned outwards, the knee bent where the fiddle neck would come down to and rise up again, she churned out tune after tune. Typically saving the best to last she proceeded to belt out the words to *Devil in the House with the Rising Sun* and stroked that instrument for all she was worth. They nearly caught alight, as did the appreciative and much inebriated audience. As if they hadn't been entertained sufficiently, the band chose to strike up again, following an encore and even again. She was smiling so much she found herself virtually laughing with joy.

The whole night was a riot, in the best of ways. There was a lock-in which everyone made the most of and eventually the band put away their instruments, the bar began to empty and she tottered off back with Tom's sister to crash at her pad.

Another time the entertainment proved to come from an entirely different source. She had been invited to a rodeo not long after she had arrived in Tamauri. Scott, his wife and their family were all there on an outing. She was taking in everything going on about her throughout the afternoon, the clowns, the cowboys and cowgirls and marvelling at their horsemanship. The day was proving to be a hot one and the crowd had grown to bursting point, with standing room only.

She was concentrating partly on the main arena, though also to the opposite side in the corral, where horses were waiting their turn to be ridden. These weren't your average nags though, these were wild, wild beasts and one had more spirit in him than his owner had vouched for. The corral was built to contain the horses. It had high sides, so that you could only just make out the tips of the tallest horses ears, if they were pricked and alert. She could see it was robust with strong wood and rivets. Certainly it was built for a purpose.

As she was starting to pay a little more attention to this one particular wild stallion, she realised he was getting increasingly more agitated. He started to rock back and forth, not dissimilar to a child's rocking horse, but this feisty animal was no toy. Now he was up on his haunches and pawing the air with his front hooves. One of the cowboys must have been yanking at a rope attached to a head collar on the horse, because she could see its head being tugged desperately up and down. He was whinnying now and almost screeching, not out of excitement or exhilaration, but with fear and anger it seemed.

She could hardly take her eyes off the scene before her. But looking about quickly to see who else was witnessing the scene she suddenly realised a whole heap of people were running frantically for cover. She turned back again to see the situation worsening. She could hear a number of the other cowboys shouting orders to each other and the horse, though their voices were being lost in the din of the panic-stricken crowd.

Looking about her once more she spotted Scott. He had been standing way off on a high point, away from the potential danger, cupping his hands over his mouth like a loud speaker and straining to make himself heard. She got the message anyway and shot up to where he stood, amidst the petrified women and children and the steadfast protective men.

By now, any efforts the professionals were making to calm the horse down had been to no avail. With all the energy left in those well-toned muscles, the animal went back on his hind legs again and with one attempt leapt clear of the corral.

It was scary, truly terrifying. The horse was bolting, erratically about the desperately panic-stricken crowd. People were fleeing in every direction. Some had taken refuge in the local ambulance parked up to one side, but when the horse looked as if it was heading straight for them, someone screamed an order at them to get out and take cover somewhere else. A few people in the crowd were tripping over themselves, trying to keep clear of the danger that was hurtling about amongst them. By now those who knew half enough about horses were attempting to be the hero of the hour. Lunging at the horse, first one side and then the other, they only succeeded in making the horse more agitated still.

Whether it ran out of steam or some cowboy merely got lucky with a lasso, the horse was caught either way and placed in its own corral with sentries in position astriding the top of it. Just like most eventful scenarios out here, things quickly got back to normal and the rodeo show resumed. She didn't know about anyone else, but the whole thing had definitely taken the puff out of her; it had been exhilarating.

Tom's farm wasn't without its own amusements. Once he had shot off in the morning, on his quad bike. It had bemused her that they were used out here as a sheep dog substitute. Here where most things seemed to be forty or fifty years behind the times, in terms of technology. Anyway, Tom was young enough and fit enough to use one, unlike Scott, who looked as if he had been born in the saddle.

She was left keeping house and was making some headway in clearing the vegetable garden of weeds, stones the size of her hands and general scrub. Everything was prepared for lunch when she heard a cry, followed by shouts and expletives. Clearly, something was up.

Running outside and tripping over the rake she had forgotten to store away, she peered across Tom's land in every direction. The shouting and yelling continued. She began to get worried, thinking the worst. What could she do? She ought to have some sort of plan. Commonsense told her he would probably be fine, considering he was still making noises.

She stared and ran in the direction the sounds were coming from. Past the docile bull under his tree, beside the heifers and amongst the hundreds of sheep which grazing one minute were sent scattered the next, only to join up together in a line, as sheep do.

Another time Tom had taken her on the back of the quad bike around the farm. That was during the episode when he seemed a bit keen on her. She was carried away still with the romance of it all, staying there with him, almost like his woman. Now she was going to save his life. Surely he would appreciate her more after that, allow himself to demonstrate to her just how deep his feelings ran for her, at least now they were alone.

There he stood. He was knee deep in thick, wet mud, tall, un-kept grassland about him. Still screaming. She must have looked confused, because he seemed to be cross and not just with his predicament. Then she spotted the problem. Lying there, half in the muddy creek with him and resting painfully against his inner thigh and knee, the quad bike, engine still revving. She realised the face on Tom was a grimace. The bike must have weighed a ton and now, mingled with the mud and filth was evidence of blood, seeping from a gape in Tom's leg, just where a section of the machine must have scraped itself onhim.

This was one of those times when she wished she didn't care quite so much about her appearance. She knew anyone else in that situation, who lived the farming life, would have been in there, up to their own eyes in the muck. But her immediate thoughts were of her clothes, her hair. Tom shot her a look and barked something about helping him to shift the bike off him. She came to her senses, paused for a second or two to assess the situation. Didn't they say if an object was penetrating a wound, not to dislodge or remove it in case you might cause a major bleed? When she studied the area more closely, whilst edging down and across to Tom's aid, she calmed herself and her nerves, safe in the knowledge the injury was seemingly superficial. With all her might she heaved the bike away and off from the damaged limb. She knew if she hadn't there was neither no one else out with them for miles to help, nor could she expect any more affection or even friendship from her boss than previously.

He was appreciative though, but his mind was focused on the practicalities. The quad bike was an expensive piece of kit and with the price of wool not matching his outgoings as closely as he would have liked, Tom was as mad and frustrated as the next farm worker in his position.

Once he was out of the mud with the bike, Tom was off back to his yard to fetch a vehicle, suitable to take the machine back to see if he could fix it himself. He stayed in a sulk for the remainder of the day, but that was entertainment enough for her. What a child! She tried to understand the worrying situation he was in. Though not being responsible for the upkeep of the farm in reality, she couldn't feel too concerned. Also, she was only too aware Tom spent every spare penny he earned on his polo excursions, off to foreign parts and his foreign girlfriends. She couldn't help laughing inwardly at the image of him, out there in that sticky muddle. That was precisely what his life was like and especially his love life. Then most probably, she was only serving to muddle him further. They weren't any good for each other, he was right there.

Christmas followed the final polo tournament and the Ball. She spent it with a fellow Brit, who was a player, not a groom like herself. Maybe it was this difference, this contrast in their positions, or the fact that he was an officer in the army back home, but he was by far the bossiest person she had met, not purely out in Tamauri, but anywhere.

Initially, he had been enormous fun, a good fun guy who flirted with the girls and got on well with the men. He was confident with the ponies. He certainly knew all there was to know about polo, but the negatives were his weight and his arrogance. Knowing she wasn't the most competent of riders, she knew all the same he shouldn't fall off as often as he did, unless that was the daredevil in him. Even so, the way he bounced when he came out the side of his ride was close to hysterical. He really had a very large arse, if she could be forgiven for thinking such. Combined with his piggy-like eyes, he made a fine sight and yet so arrogant, very fitting.

Still, he had his uses. When she had lost her confidence almost entirely following the fall with the grey, he had taken it upon himself to encourage her back on top. She was enormously grateful to him and when he offered her the chance to have some company over the Christmas festivities, she pretty much jumped at the chance.

He had really gone to town in an effort to bring the tradition of it all to the two of them, alone out there on the stud where he was based. They had a small chicken between them with the obligatory vegetables and even a miniature Christmas cake. He insisted on cooking everything, even producing his own gravy and demonstrating to her, step by step, how to be the master chef that he protested to be. He was clever in the kitchen and good company, when the mood took him. Sometimes he was in a filthy mood.

The mood swings, flickering moments of affection, a growing deepening friendship, lasted all over Christmas Day. By Boxing Day they were off on a trip he must have planned months before, typically.

He drove them up the coast to a place where he had been told they might catch a glimpse of some whales on a clear day. Pulling over, they looked out through the car's window to the cove below them and some way out there they saw these graceful mammals. They were transfixed for a while together, both speechless.

Then they got out of the car for a better look and in the excitement of sharing that scene together, he pulled her down onto the grass with him, up on that cliff top and pushed her skirt up and over her hips. She blinked frantically up at his serious face, which instantly broke into a smile of pure wickedness. This was fun! She allowed him to find his way about inside her knickers. Then she was raising her knees up for him and he was entering her. All about them was the sound of the sea and the creatures which moved with it, inward and outward. It was a comfort, tranquilising.

Someone was laughing. More than one person was having a fine time chortling away and then it dawned on them. The laughter was due to their antics. They were being watched. A few passing ramblers were enjoying the entertainment. Thankfully they looked to be of a similar age to themselves and did not seem offended. She thought to cover herself up, to jump up, but something naughty in her made her stop and let them enjoy the scene. They were erotic, so desperate for each other they had ignored convention.

She was not so foolish to appreciate this man she was with was taking full advantage of an opportunity for a quick roll with her. He might well have thought up the whole thing, Christmas lunch, the romantic drive, the whales, although even he couldn't have staged that. Still, she was getting something out of this too. She was learning. You could play the men at their own game, just as long as you kept your wits about you and never allowed yourself to take any of them too seriously.

They continued their journey, stopping here and there. There were some delightful places to visit and she thanked him and left him, at the end of it, with mixed emotions and memories to match.

New Year was precisely as she would have wanted it to turn out. She was in good company with Tom's sister and her chums, hanging out in their favourite local, half cut before the night had really got into full swing. Like the Ball, the whole episode, virtually, was a merry blur but with the additional privilege of not being required to work the ponies the next day.

With the polo season over, even the ponies were entitled to a rest.

With the New Year, she slowly started to piece together what had transpired in the months leading up to it. She had discovered who were her genuine friends, whose company was actually worse than no company at all. That allegedly her boss would be more than happy if she was back in England, rather than crushing his style, hanging about his heels the way she did at times. That every member of Tom's family was well aware of her affections towards him, of their tense relationship and the interesting journey she had enjoyed over the Christmas break. She wasn't such a stranger to them any more. If anything, they held far too much ammunition on her. Thankfully, she felt she could trust them to live and let live. If you didn't provide them with the gossip, got on with your job and did it well, you were alright in their eyes. Better than that, if you laughed at their jokes and funny stories. Sometimes they made her feel relaxed, at others, somewhat nervous for certain, she was at her best when Tom was off the scene.

The weeks and months went on like this and eventually the time came when she genuinely needed to leave and get herself home.

Unexpectedly, they held a surprise leaving party, with a cake, presents, the works. There were tears from the girls, Tom's sister and herself realising maybe what had grown between them. She was moved, more than she had imagined and when she had to say goodbye at the airport, the tears were positively uncontrollable.

She should have flown on to Fiji, but there was a problem with the flight and she went straight to Los Angeles airport instead. She hadn't much money anyway, since Tom had reneged on his original promise and it was left to Scott and his wife to recompense her. Knowing she had nowhere to live and no job to go to at home, she knew she would have to be sensible, frugal even. The good times were behind her for the time being.

The years went by frighteningly quickly. She had relationships, jobs whenever she could land them and managed to keep a roof over her head somehow. There were a medley of people she surrounded herself with, as often as possible, in an effort not to get lonely. But eventually she had to listen to herself and follow her heart back to Belindi.

THE BALL
AND THE BUMP

Towards the end of her University days in Scotland she agreed to attend a Ball along with a crowd of good friends. Having been to several before she knew what to expect and was greatly looking forward to a good time being had by all. She was proud of her choice of dress, a scarlet red number with big, puffy-out short sleeves, cut just above the knee. It was one of those dresses in which she felt safe; there was always a chance she could be thrown or dropped to the floor, in which case there was the probability that she would be revealing her knickers to all and sundry. As for her breasts, though, they weren't going anywhere, which made for a change!

It was winter and winters in Scotland were bleak, with this one being no exception. A blizzard was blowing, visibility was virtually non-existent and she was glad she hadn't been roped into driving. It was likely her mates were aware by now that she didn't make the safest of drivers at nightfall, something she held in common with her mother.

At that time she was sharing a cottage out in the sticks where life was rough but good fun most of the time. It meant that they had to make their own way to and from University. Now, squeezed into the back of a very second-hand Metro with several other party hopefuls she tried to get a glimpse of the outside in an effort to see where on their route they had got to. When the car lurched to a halt, everyone was thrown forwards, herself almost being impaled on the gear stick, then back again with a thump against the PVC seats. It was steamy in there now, condensation speckled the glass in competition with the snowflakes from outside. The owner and driver had pumped the heating system full, but with the joking and jostling it was stifling now.

"We're going to get some money from the cash point. Does anyone need any for themselves?" came a deep, urgent voice from outside.

It made her jump, recognising it as her boyfriend who had been travelling in another car ahead of them. The thought, ridiculously, hadn't crossed her mind. Of course she was going to need some cash. They had paid in advance for their tickets but that only included one bottle of red and white per table of eight. She had to think quickly. What was her bank balance like these days? Not good. Maybe she could switch to water once her share of the wine had run out? Not likely. There was only one thing to do - live a little.

"Yep. Could you get some out for me, please?" she asked into the darkness.

"How much do you want?"

"Twenty. Here's my card and my PIN number is the same as the cat's birthday, remember?"

"Okay, come on, hand it over. I'm freezing my bollocks off out here."

"Sorry, sorry. There you go." She leant over the passenger to her right and poked the credit card through a small gap in the window.

They waited a few minutes, the engine running, drowning out the words of a tune on the car radio, but she knew what they were and started singing them as loud as she dared. The others joined in, louder still and before they knew it the car was rocking along with the seven of them, all squashed in together.

"It won't take it," came a loud, booming, aggressive voice from the blackness again.

She jumped, quite shaken, then collecting herself she called out the PIN number in case he hadn't remembered it properly.

"Are you sure?" he asked.

"Of course I'm sure," she replied in astonishment.

Great! He hadn't even begun to drink and already his mood was turning sour. Watching him from the warmth of the car she felt guilty. Perhaps she ought to have gone out there herself? He was stooped over the hole in the wall, his great winter coat billowing about his long, slender legs, black in his suit. He looked dashing in spite of the grimace on his face. Why did he get so angry, especially with her? She saw him turn round and trudge back in the unrelenting snow and the murky sludge about his polished shoes, a scowl upon his face. Her heart began to pound, her shoulders were hunched up with tension. Any attempts at a sing-song had faltered. The mood was now one of dread. Most of them were aware of his temper, one or two had experienced it first hand for all she knew. Please God make him happy again, the life and soul if he had a mind to, that was the alternative and her obvious choice.

"Okay. Does anyone fancy going to a Ball tonight?"

"Me!" came the roar from the car.

"All right then, move up, I'm getting in there with you."

"No! There's no room, get out you're squashing my tits."

There was more shoving, pushing and laughter as she'd hoped, then they were away again; the Metro back-firing with the effort.

When they arrived there was a flurry of arms and legs as everyone fought to get in out of the cold and head for the booze. They found their table and studied the order of things in relation to the dancing, or reeling as it was termed here. There were a few of which she thought she could remember quite a few of the steps to. Now, if one of those gorgeous men in their sexy Black Ties or, failing that, kilts, would oblige her and ask her to join them on the floor, that would be grand. She kept her head down beginning to feel slightly deflated as the other girls about her were being scooped up, one after another. Most were in fits of giggles, disguising their embarrassment. Finally, and not before too long, a pair of hairy and incredibly muscular legs approached her.

"Can you Strip the Willow?"

"I'll give it a go. I think I can remember what to do, so long as you don't spin me too fast."

They both headed towards the dance floor, leaving a table of empty glasses and half-finished bottles of champagne and wine - most of which she had to admit had found their way her end. She gave a friendly smile at her fellow reelers and lined up for the start of the dance, already feeling giddy with excitement and alcohol. The music began and they were off. One lad with his lass made their way down a tunnel of other couples, clapping in time to the tune, then back again to twist and turn and spin, spin, spin.

The band comprised an obligatory piper, some jock with the most enormous sporran she had laid her eyes on and a white beard to match, was on the accordion, whilst another played a mean fiddle and called out the steps in an audible yet calming tone. It was peculiar to her how so many drunken men and women could be kept so captivated by the music. It was as though hearing it enhanced them. They were almost being controlled by the rhythm. Maybe it was sobering to not want to embarrass themselves by making a mistake?

A few dances and drinks later and any inhibitions remaining were fading alongside their visibility. She wasn't capable of deciding if the hall was spinning from the dancing or the fizz. So that was why they called it Scottish reeling?

It was later, still, when she was being spun about the room by a rather good-looking chap from Dundee when it happened. It was a moment of madness in hindsight. She had allowed everything about the night to go to her head and leaning back as far as their arms could stretch, daring and yet trusting each other at the same time not to let one another go, they spun like a wheel on its side. Just like anyone would tell you, it really did all happen in slow motion. She remembered turning or rather spinning in a clockwise rotation, arms outstretched, fingers locked with her dancing partner. Then another girl, spinning with equal force and velocity but anti-clockwise, came careering towards her. What happened next would have a huge impact on the rest of the night and the next morning. The other female dancer smashed her shoulder into her target's temple, bang and bang again as she crashed down on the floor. The worse-case scenario during a reel had transpired.

There seemed to be some few seconds that passed that were a blur, if non-existent to her as she tried to come to her senses. Quickly, she remembered the naked shoulder rushing towards her head. Simultaneously the length, or more relevantly the shortness, of her dress had diverted attention from the throb, throb of her head injury as the red silk lay there crumpled up around her waist like a pool of blood. Frantically, she tugged at it under her bruised pride, looking about her on all sides in the vain hope no one had seen what had just happened.

Amazingly everyone was still happily reeling away in their own little world of wine and merry-making. Several couples were obviously flirting with each other now. At the far side of the wall, unbelievably, one girl stood with her back to a pillar, obviously encouraging some man to help himself to the contents of her knickers, in full public view. Even by her own standards they were drawing far too much of the wrong attention to themselves, judging from the perverse looks on people's faces. In fact they were drawing quite a crowd, which gave her the opportunity to pick herself up from the floor and straighten herself out.

Whoosh. Help. Someone stop this room from turning. A medical student, who coincidentally shared a cottage with her and her boyfriend, seemed to be thrashing his way through the throng of voyeurs. Having spotted her he instantly recognised an opportunity to let his First Aid knowledge shine.

"Are you all right? What happened? Oh, Christ your head!" he blurted out through the stench of vino and a few cheap malts.

She managed to prevent a criticism coming out about the state he was in, reminding herself of her own incapacitating condition.

"I think my head has just made contact with someone's shoulder."

"Come with me. Are you all right to walk? Here, here, take my arm. God, you're a bit unsteady on your feet old girl. That's it, you can do it, this way. Don't worry about them, it's you I'm worried about. Okay, try and sit down here, careful now, steady, steady. Someone get her some water. Here now, try and look at my hand. How many fingers am I holding up?"

"Three, no four."

"Well done. You're doing brilliantly."

"Don't you think someone should call an ambulance?"

"Yes, look use my mobile."

"No, wait a minute. I don't think we need to panic. How are you feeling now? Can you see double?"

"No, I don't think so but you're not looking very clear. That's probably down to the alcohol though."

"Yeah, you're probably right. You silly thing!"

"She'll be all right, won't she?"

"Yes, of course she will. You'll be all right, won't you?"

"Definitely. I'm feeling better already. Who's for a dance, anybody?"

"That's the spirit. Can you stand now? Up you get."

After that she was well past caring. The booze, the bump and the Ball, everything and everyone went to her head in as many ways as she could have imagined. The band eventually came to a standstill and one of the party revellers doubled up as a voluntary DJ to help see them through to the morning. She felt she was experiencing another one of those magnificent moments when there was an intense feeling of happiness oozing from all about her. They were as one. The acoustics in the ballroom bounced off the wood-panelled walls and age-old oil paintings of distinguished past professors and lecturers. Below her lay a dusty wooden floor, sprawled with screwed up messy napkins, cigarette ends, the odd used match and a lilac pashmina distressingly stained with what appeared to be the raspberry Pavlova. A truly wonderful, lasting feeling, until she ventured off to the Ladies.

"Oh, shit! What happened to you?"

"Oh, I bumped into someone. I'm fine, really."

"No way. Have you seen your face?"

"Look at her face everyone."

"Let me see, oh my God."

"You should go to the hospital."

"Didn't someone get you an ambulance?"

"Dial 999 somebody."

The voice, and the panic, the concern, the urgency came from all directions about her. She looked in the mirror to see what all the fuss was about.

"Oh, shit! I hadn't realised."

Staring back at her was a person only just recognisable, even to its owner. What she knew before as her blue eyes were framed with bruising which was so swollen there was barely any evidence of a bridge to her nose. Even her eyebrows and her forehead were blown up out of all sense of proportion. She looked like one of those very unfortunate victims of abuse whose faces sometimes appeared on late night crime prevention programmes.

"I'm fine, really. I'm fine. I don't need an ambulance. Please don't make a fuss. It's nothing."

"Oh, come on. Look at yourself. No I think you should come with me."

"Did you get knocked unconscious?"

"No, I don't think so, I ...."

"She could have delayed concussion though, couldn't she? You could have delayed concussion."

"Yes, my brother had that. You have to be so careful."

"Yes, I know a friend of my cousin's and he had concussion and a few days later he collapsed at work with a brain haemorrhage or something."

"Oh no. What happened to him? Was he all right?"

"No, he died, just like that. He was only twenty-one."

"Oh shit. Imagine that. That's not right is it? His parents must have been really upset. I mean, they're not meant to live longer than their children are they, you know. It's not right is it?"

"No. Life's a bitch."

"And then you die."

"Oh nightmare! Hey, can anyone let me have a tampon, I've just got my bloody period."

"Sure, hold on. I think I've got one in my purse somewhere, yeah. Here you go. Can you reach?"

"Cheers mate. You're a life saver."

"I know."

"Look, I'm all right honestly. Don't make a fuss. My friend is a medical student and he's already checked me over."

"Yeah, I bet he has!"

"Yeah, any excuse, hey?"

"No really, he's done that test with his fingers and I'm all right. I don't remember blacking out or anything."

"Well, if you're sure. But first thing tomorrow you should get someone to take you to A&E and have a proper check-up, okay?"

"Okay, okay. Thanks for your concern."

"That's all right. See you in there."

"Rachel, are you finished yet?"

"Hold on, hold on. I'm coming."

"Mmm, that sounds familiar. Look, hurry up. I think I'm onto a promise tonight."

"Oh come on! I thought we agreed we weren't going to be on the pull."

"That was before I met Mr Gorgeous."

"And what does Mr G do with himself when he's not reeling?"

"Well, that's what I aim to find out!"

"Ha, ha!"

The giggling girls hurriedly shoved and pushed each other back to the dance floor, flicking their eyelashes and thrusting their chests out at the men. The DJ pumped the volume up still further and the room was lifting.

University life seemed to almost pass her by. In the space of four years she somehow managed to hold on to a long-term relationship, just, take up rowing and come away with a degree, miraculously. Not that the studying was ever worth the hassle as far as she could make out, jobs were scarce. In fact she thanked her lucky stars she had been given an opportunity to spend part of her education boarding in one of the country's top private schools. It was this asset to her curriculum vitae that was pulling in the work. Certainly it had impressed her boss at an estate agents, where she found herself employed as their receptionist. Front of house, he had informed her. She would be giving the company's first impression to perspective clients and other 'POIs' (people of importance) as he liked to abbreviate them and seemingly everything else.

Initially, she almost enjoyed herself there. It beat scraping a living working as a volunteer, or 'angel' as she and the other girls were referred to, at the auctioneering house. How patronising! Well, she soon saw through them. With the exception of one lovely lady who took her under her wing and allowed her to take up residence in her delightful flat in smart Bragminton, virtually rent-free,. everyone seemed to be out for themselves, for what they could get from life, how quickly and how far up the career and social ladders they could get, no matter what.

With regard to the other girls and boys she worked with day-to-day, side-by-side at the same level, she could tell who was after a bigger piece of the action. They wanted to impress, constantly, and in any shape or form. The majority though just tried to see it through the long, sometimes tedious, often gruelling day. Then they were off to the staff room to climb into their going out gear and quick-smart it out of there, off to the nearest gathering of squawking, moaning, wittering, disadvantaged, insular types for the night and no doubt the next morning, if they had a mind to. She wouldn't join them for their merry-making. Though when she realised they never invited her anyway, she felt terrible, vulnerable and lonely.

Her reaction would be to shirk off those feelings and kid herself that there was more to life. She knew, she had seen it out there for herself. Instead, she would make her way back to Bragminton, walking all the way, so as to cut costs and save the money for her supper.

There was one other friendly face, aside from her landlady. He came in the form of a law student who lived just a stone's throw from her. She met him in the local garage all-night shop, buying all the broadsheets going. They got talking, worked out they were neighbours, of a similar age and background and took it from there.

He gave her something to look forward to. He was good company, always ready with a fascinating story, normally of people he had come across and the case studies he had taken on. Generally, he wasn't able or allowed to confide in her any personal details of clients and as much as she desperately wanted him to trust her, she respected him for his professionalism.

So they would share a cheap meal, sometimes home-cooked. When they were feeling flush, a bottle of wine to complement the food and to remind themselves they were adults working and living in a civilised society, where they ought to be entitled to enjoy themselves. To think of what she had become accustomed to in Belindi.

She shuddered to think of how unappreciative of life she had become, she was spoilt. Then again, she could see she clearly wasn't in Belindi now, nor any other undeveloped or developing country gone awry. Sure there were allegations of corruption within her own country's government, but she couldn't believe it would reach the heights it could in places she had stayed in.

The auctions were exciting, exhilarating really. She got involved in several sales, though it was the Old Masters that generally saw her coming into her own. There was one occasion when everything appeared to be running as smoothly as it could. It amused her the way there was clearly such mayhem behind the scenes, while out at the front of house all was serene, peaceful, yet crammed to the rafters with expectation, hesitancy and greed. When the sale reached mid-way, the auctioneer announced the arrival of their greatest piece yet. Truly, it was awesome. An inspiration to all who cast their eyes over the sumptuous colours. Those who were blessed with being seated close enough could take in the incredible brushstrokes, that intricate frame, the painstaking, heartfelt, smoothness with which the multitude of colours had been laid down beside each other. At a distance they conjured up the forms of some Bacchanalian scene, a pastoral image in the background, some Arcadian form of a ruin to one side, nymphs and the coursing sea, rushing in between a rugged outcrop to the other. There was an audible intake of breath from everyone.

At this point a man stepped into the room, breaking the spell. He excused himself and his three companions, all smartly dressed in their pinstriped suits. Announcing himself to be an expert, he promptly announced the work of art to be nothing more than a fake, albeit an attractive one. There was another intake of breath, sharper than the first. After a brief pause she was aware of a commotion behind and around her amongst her fellow porters and the auctioneer was motioning for the security guard. Then things spiralled into a real hullabaloo and now she felt the tables had turned. It was the turn of the bosses to be on their toes, to look out, watch their backs, not the underlings like herself. Someone was going to be for the high-jump and she was going to enjoy the inevitable gossip which could no doubt proceed from the events. What a shock for everyone. How funny!

When her all too short contract expired and there were no offers of further employment, she merely took work where she could get it. That included the estate agents. There too she found herself amongst a mixed bag of personalities. One character was so offensive towards her she began to wonder if she needed to toughen up a little, or a lot. In the end she refused to change for the sake of fitting in and the culmination was her losing her job, though purely momentarily.

Whilst clearing her desk, she took one final call, as per her job description, answering the phone as the dutiful, conscientious receptionist she was. The person at the other end turned out to be her future boss. The reason for the call was to offer her a job she had applied for. She remembered how she had felt so impish, sneaking out in her lunch break to meet up with her hoped for potential boss to be.

It turned out to have been the best thing she could have done for herself. The position was definitely a promotion in her eyes, to negotiator. A huge improvement on her current measly salary and initially a much kinder, sympathetic and humourous crew with whom to work. Life, as she saw it, seemed to be taking a more positive turn, for now at least.

Work was good. At times hectic, but this time she was thriving on it. No one seemed to be exploiting her. If anything she was her own boss. Fabulous! They had fun, a lot of laughs together, especially as the weekend drew nearer. For her, Fridays were the best. She would mentally stop working at around five, one hour officially before she ought to, though no one seemed to care. Otherwise, she found them rather willing and able to partake of a bottle of wine, courtesy of their boss, who doubled up as the company accountant. Given his demanding role, this was generally about the only time she could see him relax and share a joke or two with them, to tell a tall story even.

The person who really made a difference to how her day would go, the week even, worked just behind her. She was her superior, but unfortunately this would go to her head at times and she could be quite arrogant, aggressive, perhaps if the mood took her and things weren't going to plan, then slightly offensive. She had heard worse, but why she so often felt as if she was the catalyst to these outbursts she couldn't make out.

It was in fact not the case at all. After some time, having worked together for almost two years, her partner in crime in their small, yet significant lettings empire, opened up over a second bottle of Pinot Grigio. It wasn't her at all, it was all about a man. Any inadequacies, lateness, sickies, incompetences she had been guilty of had only served to worsen a frame of mind, worsening by the minute in correlation with any calls or e-mails picked up by her love-struck colleague in the corner.

There were other relationships within the job place which were mostly worthwhile. One friend she made there was good for a laugh, if nothing short of hilarious. But she had made her own mark by then with her efforts to meet her margin.

On a bright, crisp spring morning, she found herself faced with that worst of dilemmas, when she had accompanied a gentleman to a property. It was a Saturday, when she normally would be helping out in the sales department. Unusually, the member of staff responsible for the client had made a special request of her that she showed him around this house. It wasn't until she had tried each and every key in her possession that she suspected she wasn't going to gain entry. That was the moment she spotted the side gate in the garden at the rear. The next problem she faced was the realisation that the gate in question was over six feet in height. Still, unfazed, she was adamant she wasn't going to let her team down and without a moment's hesitation she scaled the obstacle, hot-footing it up and over into the outside space behind. Once there, she had presumed she would be able to open the until now locked gate from the other side. Yet as she was on the verge of shifting the bolt across, from out of its shaft, the face of her companion appeared over the top. He was enquiring as to whether she might move aside to give him better access?

As it turned out, the property was a prize gem, with more space then any biased description could portray. The interior wasn't disappointing either, though it still left a margin for improvement. The client was as excited as herself and before the end of the month, she was informed he had made an acceptable offer and she could expect to be remunerated for her trouble. This aside, the story of her scaling the heights of her profession, surpassing all expectations of an estate agent, conquering anxieties and a six foot garden gate to secure a deal, went the rounds. Even when she left the job and returned at a later stage on a temporary and part-time basis, the tale came back to haunt her, in the nicest way.

She found she didn't mind being the centre of attention. It was rather flattering. Consequently, she began to get involved in amateur dramatics, joining a society a stone's throw from her flat in Bragminton. The people there were extremely welcoming, real luvvies in the making. That season they were putting on their interpretation of the musical *Carousel*. Short of a dancer and keen to boost the contribution of the chorus line, they auditioned her without her prior knowledge. Then they kitted her out with a pair of ballet shoes half a size too big and a gaudy costume that emphasised her bust.

Rehearsals were going better than any of them could expect, even the props manager had succeeded in delivering the goods. Things couldn't be better. She had a fantastic time, a superb work-life balance, finally.

They were congratulating themselves following a marvellous dress rehearsal and looking forward, surprisingly she thought, to the first night's performance. It came around sure enough and, surprisingly to her again, everything went smoothly, swimmingly well in fact, according to her fellow thespians. Life couldn't be more different, in contrast with the boys school she had left behind in Belindi. On the final night she joined the rest of the cast in a celebratory drinks party backstage. There wasn't a dry eye in the house, though the same could not be said for the copious bottles of champagne they had managed to get through. Everyone came together for a group hug, the air was kissed a few dozen times, lights switched off, alarms set and doors locked, all except the one through to the costumes department, quite why no one knew. But when the fire brigade had at last managed to put out those vicious flames and had dampened down the smouldering embers of the last remains of the stage curtains, they had a few questions to ask.

Arson was suspected and she found herself being questioned and quizzed as thoroughly as those fire fighters had quenched the thirst of that menacing fire. Like most of the others, thankfully, she had witnesses to excuse her from any blame. However, it turned out one of the stagehands, a kid really, probably only just out of school, had started it. Got in with the wrong crowd perhaps, a cry for help, mental health difficulties, she didn't have the answers. What a shame though, such waste, it was sickening.

For a few months at least, leading up to that Christmas and briefly over the New Year period, she kept in touch with the play group. Eventually, some moved on to bigger and better things, she hoped. Until there were only one or two whose names and numbers she would feel she could call on her for friendship and maybe some fun?

Of these was a girl who coincidentally shared a passion for horses too. They spent most of their spare time right through that winter and the next two seasons. They were good company for each other, quite different in their personalities it seemed, but they complemented each other, most of the time. As summer drew to a close they made a flash decision between themselves to pick a package holiday somewhere with a warmer climate, Spain.

The Spanish coastline where they landed was much more attractive than they had thought, considering how little they had coughed up for the deal. Not only that, but their hotel was fairly special too and their luck didn't seem to end there either. When they were eventually allowed into their hotel, which they had no prior knowledge of anyway, being allocated on arrival, they discovered they were in the penthouse. Things didn't stop there. They found a great wine bar, staggering distance away, which was serving up free tapas after ten with every bottle of Sangria. Then they both came up trumps in two of the hotel's games competitions, coming away with a six-pack each of the local brew. They didn't care, the more the merrier, it was a holiday after all.

That was when this so-called friend lost the plot one night, arguably having drunk more that time than on previous occasions. They were lying in their respective beds, complaining of mosquitoes when from absolutely nowhere whatsoever, came a sudden torrent of abuse, directed systematically at her room mate. Why this fellow holidaymaker should feel the need to throw up all that anger and bitterness in her direction, she couldn't fathom. All she knew was it definitely was not deserved, and come the morning, she was going to make sure she fixed it so she could be on the next flight out of there.

Alcohol appears to play strange tricks with the mind at times. By the following day they seemed to be back on a level footing, reading from the same hymn sheet – whatever one would call it. She didn't make any kind of comment about the previous night's events, how she had been subjected to hours of insults and expletives. Could it have been because she believed she deserved some of it or, more likely, because she didn't want to lose another friend, like she had lost Samuel?

They saw out the remainder of the break in Spain together and then work and this excuse and that excuse meant they lost touch after a short while. Only when a mutual friend meant their coming together in company was inevitable, did they have the chance to swap stories. She was alright with that. She felt they had enough in common, had shared things together, which meant theirs was the type of friendship which would last over and beyond most events life had to throw at them.

THE BOAT TRIP

There was a man she met when she was living in Bragminton. This one never seemed to let her down, nor put her down come to that. Kind, intelligent, caring, loving even. With all those positive attributes he only served to keep her attention more acutely by his adventurous nature. This they shared and eventually he was to capture her heart as well.

They shared stories – good and bad – of the people, places and things they had met with over the years. He had climbed a mountain, in the literal sense, whilst she had tales of her own courage and commitment, both of which she agreed could be substituted for naivety and stubbornness.

When they had enough money between them, they would take advantage of any last-minute deal that came their way. Each scanning the internet for cheap flights, bargains, any which way just to satisfy their mutual hunger to explore. One such trip took them to the Mediterranean where they found themselves staying in a hotel on the beach for the price of a week's shopping back home.

It was low season and therefore, being almost deserted, they basked by the near-empty hotel pool, strolled along clean and clear soft, sandy beaches and contemplated life with the constant turning of the tide. Having sampled the local everything, they agreed to venture out further than the boundaries of the hotel and town perimeters. Finally, they learnt of a local travel agency that catered for excursions, as expected in such places.

The boat floated before them, seemingly nattering with similar sized vessels, flotillas, fishing boats and the like, nodding at them in agreement. They flip-flopped their way down a gangplank and with a kindly helping hand from one of the crew landed themselves a space on a narrow wooden bench on the starboard side. Other committed holidaymakers were striding in the direction of the same. Somehow everyone squeezed in and they were cast off.

They congratulated themselves on their choice, marvelling at the faultless sky above them. The boat slid over the silken waters, further and further out from the shore, leaving their hotel far off in the distance. But just as they were squinting their eyes at one coastline, unexpectedly another slowly emerged in their sights behind them.

"You can take a swim here if anyone fancies it. The waters are a perfect temperature in these parts ... but watch out for jellyfish ... oh, and sharks of course."

The boat trippers laughed in unison, then realising the Captain was serious about the swimming at least, one or two began to readily strip. They glanced about them at the array of swimwear and feeling they were rapidly becoming the minority gave in and leapt off the boat into the emerald waves below.

"This is no fun at all," she complained.

"Oh come on, it's lovely once you get going."

"The only place I'm going is back on board the boat."

"Oh no you don't. Come here you tigress."

"Get off me. I'm not staying here, I'm freezing."

"Oh, don't leave me here, please. I might get attacked by a giant shark-eating jellyfish or man-eating seaweed or something worse."

"Well, at least you would be safe from the man-eating shark."

"True."

"Okay. How about last one to the island gets the drinks?"

"You're on."

They reached the warm sands in less time than she expected, stumbling from the water and righting themselves as they laughed at their efforts. She was holding her side with the fun of it all and felt they were in a little paradise all of their own. But that clearly was not going to be the case. Quickly coming back to reality as she righted herself and looked up, there looking back at her was a hoard of fellow holidaymakers. Most people were dressed appropriately, one or two had gone topless, both sexes and a few older couples were fully clothed even in the sizzling heat.

She cast her gaze around the bay, taking in the pleasing scenery – the flowers, which were totally unexpected, though not as much as the bull that now stood no more than fifty yards to her right! Nobody was saying a word, but then that didn't really surprise her. She wondered if perhaps she was the only one who had spotted it? This great big, jet-black, terribly cross-looking bull. She conjured up a memory of Tom's bull under the tree. It was a bull for Christ's sake! Wasn't anyone going to do anything? The animal had horns, sharp, pointy, sticking out horns and was it her mind, or was he looking at her? Maybe it was normal around here? It could be that the bull always strolled merrily across the local sandy coves? Perhaps it was a territorial thing? How should she know? She turned her attention to her travelling companion of the human variety.

"Is it my imagination or is it not the norm to have a stonking great big male cow on the beach?"

"I know. I think we would be better keeping very still."

"Not likely. Look, there's some land over there. A field or two, it must have come from there."

"What do you think you're doing?"

"Shhh! It's all right. I'm going to coax it back to its farm. It's probably frightened of us more than us of him."

"You are joking aren't you?"

"No. Now if you aren't going to help me, be quiet. You're scaring him."

"I'm scaring him?"

She moved slowly, arms spread-eagled ever closer towards the bull which thankfully was staying put for the time being.

"It's all right. I'm not going to hurt you" she told the animal, thinking all the while how brave she was, or foolish more likely. The thought occurred to her that it ought to be a man performing this act of dare-devilry. But that only served to insight her determination to take control of the situation alone. She was well aware she could be so stubborn at times.

"Go on now, off you go" she said to the bull, desperate to instil some semblance of authority in the tone of her voice.

"It's all right. Look, there's the farmer."

She took her eyes off the bull for a second or two, looking over its shoulder to a shabby looking man striding towards them. He was dressed as she would picture any farmer to be, yet with a face like thunder. How ungrateful she thought inwardly, when all she had in mind was the well being of what might be his prize possession. The farmer reached the bull and took from behind his back some sort of rope that he confidently threaded through a hoop in the bull's nose and led it around and back from where it had presumably escaped.

It was annoying the ingratitude of him, particularly when she had virtually put her life in danger and why she had done that she had no idea. The next thing that occurred to her was the ridiculous mess of the whole affair. She felt herself starting to shake again. Whether it was how frightened she had actually been, she wasn't sure, but she fell onto the beach laughing so much tears fell from her eyes and dribbled into the equally salty grains of sand before her.

A CONCLUSION

She had been back in England for quite some time, before she learnt of a position at another school in Belindi. Despite a hectic working life in London, trying to scratch a living, she had managed to keep in contact with her employer at the boys' school. She heard how one of the dormitories caught fire one night. No one knew what or who had started it, although it can't have helped having straw mattresses. She had never understood the necessity to have bars up at the windows either. The idea of those poor souls, crammed in there, at times, three to a bed, it made her shiver. Picturing them all desperate to reach the one exit, blocked with school bags, jackets, footballs, what a catastrophe, what a shameful loss, a waste. Some of them got out, but since the boys would often invite the village children in there, no one would ever have a clue as to the actual figure dead. Anyway, several of the boys were orphans, so there was no one to tell of their deaths, only the school pals they had left behind with those terrible images to fall back on.

It was a sad tale, though she learnt of more inspiring happenings too. The plans for a new co-ed school nearby had come to fruition. It was now up and running with a full complement of both staff and pupils. The fund-raisers had even managed to achieve the almost impossible in raising sufficient to have a swimming pool installed in the school grounds. She thought how remarkable a step in the right direction that was for everyone out there in Belindi and she missed the place. That was when her old boss explained the local village school needed help there too and she jumped at the opportunity.

The position was as a class teacher, though she did some netball coaching too, occasionally. The older pupils were coming up for their exams and needed support to prepare for them. Then she discovered the exams would be taking place in the same rooms she had taught them in, so now she was to be an exam invigilator too. She wondered if they would be expecting her to mark the papers as well, but as it turned out they were official in so much as there were examiners in the city, who were responsible for that at least. Apparently, sometimes completed exam papers would go missing altogether in transit. She tried to imagine how that must have felt for the child involved. It made her cross things were so messed up out here. Still, at least she had come back and was trying to help them in any way she knew.

The school was up a big hill. Naturally, they had called it *Mapati Biayti*, which meant happy sun school, since they would be the first to see the sun rise and fall each day. She had an arrangement whereby she lived back in her old digs at the boys school, down the hill in the valley, but three days a week or more one of the staff there would drive her up to Mapati Biayti and back again.

She could tell this was not an ideal scenario and put the word about that she would be willing to pay someone from her meagre salary if they would teach her to drive. There were surprisingly very few offers, in fact only the one, until she realised there weren't many people about her who could drive themselves in any case. Most of them had no need to learn, since they could either walk or cycle to their chosen destination and some seemed to simply stay put for the best part of the day. There was also the issue of money.

Of these, she would include the kitchen staff at the boys school, whom she had befriended the first time around. She remembered one incident, when she was sat there among them, helping with the chores, feeling at one with them, when a puppy came by. She thought he could have walked straight out of the final at Crufts, the famous dog show, he looked so adorable, so happy with life, fit or seemingly at least. Leaping up to get a better look at him, her head spinning with ideas of how she might be allowed to keep him, when one or two of the kitchen staff yelled at her to leave it. She was cradling the little animal already and wondering what could possibly be so bad about that, perhaps she was breaking some sort of custom she was unaware of or interfering in something or other. As it turned out, when she looked at the region they were motioning to her, she realised her error. The puppy had worms. He was riddled with them and now as her mind was thinking about this she started to notice just how bad a condition the poor mite was in. There must have been at least five ticks poking out of his forehead, fleas were racing up and down his pink tummy - bloated from the worms, and not from a good diet, and his teeth when he gnawed on her finger were in a state too. She glanced back at the women folk and gave them a smile to show her understanding and appreciation for their concern. They turned their attention back to their work. Looking about her outside the kitchen area, she noticed several stray cats, only now she wasn't so naïve she past them with caution, trying not to let them get too near her, knowing she couldn't help them.

Being an animal lover, it made her feel cruel to have such a cold attitude. But the people who lived there explained that any money had to be used on the villagers and their source of revenue, be it a cow, banana plantation or their truck, not a pet. She could understand that, she had seen sufficient at least, to appreciate that approach to life, though it was sad all the same.

So, the driving lessons began in earnest. She clambered up into the driver's seat of the school pick-up and off she went with her co-driver beside her, clutching either side of himself on his seat, as they bumped along. She seemed to fair alright on the main road, got up an enormous level of confidence off road, presumably since she couldn't harm anyone there, but then lost the plot when approaching a market stall.

There were quite a number of villagers compared to usual that day, as she thundered along the carriageway. The gears were suffering a hellish torture from her left hand, as she ground them up, down, across and through. The vehicle was picking up speed and her instructor advised her to ease her foot off the accelerator. But as they were careering towards the verge and nearing the market traders, he screamed in her ear to slow down. Slow down she did, but her lack of experience with the controls and in all the confusion of waving arms, people yelling what was most likely abuse, she lost control. The instructor grabbed the wheel and seemed to pull it towards him, which she thought to be totally the opposite way to which she believed they ought to have steered, away from the market stall and the villagers. She had got her mind around the pedals, under her feet, so that she was at least most certainly breaking at the time of impact. But that didn't stop a young lad and his bicycle almost going under the front wheels. She hit them she thought, yet incredibly, the boy emerged unscathed, pulling his bike out whilst shooting her a disgruntled look. Knowing how these people valued their possessions and the paramount importance of transportation to them, she breathed a hefty sigh of relief when she saw the bike and pickup looked untouched. The boy was clearly giving it the once over and when he glanced back up at her again, she gave him her best smile and prayed he would return with the same. He did. She thought about hopping out just momentarily to apologise, but her instructor grabbed her and stared at her, his lips pursed. She understood what he was or wasn't saying and they drove off.

Actually, she had to confess to feeling a little out of sorts following that near miss. So, just out of sight of the market traders she pulled in, more successfully this time, and clambered down. Then, just as she was about to turn around to the right and approach the other side, she caught something way off in the distance.

At first it was a dust cloud, evidence of another vehicle approaching them, or most likely more than one, as the cloud was growing now. They could hear the engines as they drew nearer. Her companion had leaped out of the passenger side and was standing aghast next to her. She spotted his amazed expression in the corner of her eye and double-took as now right before them was the President's motor car. Its little flag flapping madly, unmistakable, as it shot past them, followed by its entourage. There must have been some kind of security cover up front, but her sight was focused on that flag, the blacked out windows on the black car. Totally impractical in such a dry, dusty region, but still gleaming none the less. The President! The President! Well, that was the equivalent of seeing the Queen, wasn't it? She twisted quickly behind her to catch the tail lights diminishing up the road ahead. When it reached the brow of the hill and tipped over, that was it. She looked back at her instructor. He greeted her with the most beautiful white smile. Then quite strangely, she thought, he shook her hand. It must have been more of an honour for him, than an oddity. What a curious juxtaposition of wealth and poverty, power and powerlessness. These people had high hopes for their new leader, they had placed a great deal of faith in him, although the rest they kept for God. No one could blame them. After the disgusting episode which spilled into the civil war during the previous Presidency, any change to follow would be an improvement, at least that was what the people prayed for.

She started to think of the time she first visited the capital. Parts of the city amazed her, with the emphasis there seemed to be on consumerism. Advertising boards were plentiful, displaying westernised products. At the same time, there were bullet holes galore. Buildings had been left half standing, shelled out by bomb blasts. Where the billboards were, they were generally half hanging down, so that you could only actually read part of the name of the product, or perhaps half of the picture, the neck of a bottle of cola, a dusty mouth around the top.

Sometimes when she was travelling about with one or two other members of staff, of a similar age to herself, they would stop off somewhere for a break. There seemed to be one particular place, where the proprietor was especially welcoming. She couldn't make out what they were saying at times, since they largely spoke their own language there, which was Belinidian. Most likely because the owner of the café had no understanding of English, as opposed to them wanting to exclude her. She didn't really care. It was a chance for her to sit quietly, with no pressure to make conversation, for a change.

They always had the same things to eat and drink there, quite why she didn't know. Boiled eggs and either tea, made with milk and no water or Fanta, orangeade. Sometimes there were groundnuts too, roasted with far too much salt, but she liked them.

Maybe her fellow colleague, who always insisted on her joining him for lunch at Mapati Biayti, had made a mental note of her preferences. He had joined her on a number of occasions with the teachers from the boys school, where she stayed. Always sitting next to her up front, pushing himself against her thigh. There were many occasions when she caught him just staring at her. Even if there was something interesting up ahead of them, such as a group of fit, young girls on their bicycles, or women carrying water on their heads, the way they did so cleverly, their arms down at their sides. It was lovely the way the women wore their traditional dress all the time, cooking, farming, shopping. They were definitely a proud race and beautiful with it.

When it was time for a tea-break or lunch, or she needed to take a pee, there wasn't much choice as to where she would go. It was always to the small farmstead at the bottom of the hill, away from Mapati Biayti. There Paul, her colleague, and seemingly the only full-time teacher available, would have his little kettle on for them. It held only enough water for two cups and would be boiling away on his camping stove. Beside this would be a tiny table, for two again, laid out with a tablecloth, two plates with doilies beneath them, hand-made, and a bowl of boiled eggs, beside another of roasted nuts. They both had matching chairs, where, up at the school, most of the children had to sit on the floor. A perk of the job, or was he trying to impress her, all the time? It was uncomfortable. And that grin of his. He would switch it on, when he realised she had caught him watching her, poking his lips and those two large front teeth out at her, from under his wiry moustache. Then off again, his lips and teeth retreating back into that hairy cavern, that oversized upper lip abutting the lower. She couldn't wait to finish really and get back to work, which was defeating the object of a break.

In the humidity up in her classroom, whilst her pupils had their heads down in their books, studiously, she would find herself gazing out of the window to the side of the room. There was no glass in any of the windows, which allowed more air to circulate. It also gave her a very clear view of Paul's house. If she looked long and hard enough she could make him out, beavering around with his kettle and eggs. It would send a shiver down her spine.

He wouldn't try anything, surely? Sometimes, she wondered if she was giving off the wrong signals to him? But no, she knew there was no truth in that. She was there, pure and simply to get those children through their exams and through school. To what though? What were they all destined for? What job prospects did they have, quite frankly? She decided she would ask them.

Charmingly, their answers were as natural and obvious as any child their age – nurse, teacher, doctor, soldier. Soldier? It didn't seem to hold the same with her in their country. Their soldiers were often crooked, taking bribes, blackmailing, abusive, allegedly. At least they were paid, relatively regularly and worthwhile salaries. She recalled the wounded man with the gunshot injury, at the hospital where she was laid up for a while. The army had been accused of that, hadn't they? Weren't they meant to protect their own? The innocent at least. Maybe she had them all wrong? Perhaps that wounded man, shot up and mashed up, lying on that repulsive mattress wasn't quite so innocent after all? She thought back again to that lovely hope in her pupils' faces and cast aside her cynicisms for the time being.

She meant to be as positive thinking with regards to Paul too, though his lecherous, leering ways were starting to make her skin crawl. He had never intentionally laid a finger on her, yet she detested him, his company, those eggs. Ridiculous really. Everything seemed fine between them whenever anyone else was about, such as another teacher from the boys' school. As soon as she could see they were out of sight, with only a puff of scratchy, gritty road, scuffed up from under the back tyres to be seen, she would cringe again.

Then one morning in their usual positions about his table, milky tea in hand, eyes glazed over, head turned away from his, away off towards her classroom, he asked her something. She heard him clear enough the first time, but thought to herself that if she asked him to say whatever it was again, by some miracle he would say something entirely different. That he wouldn't be asking her to marry him again. Paul had an irritating way of murmuring after the end of each sentence. The fact he felt the need to exercise this habit once more now, made his proposal even more, well annoying. How could this be happening to her? How utterly preposterous that he should be sitting there, expecting there might be some possibility that she would accept his offer.

She thought she might be sick. She was going to be sick. Running out from the room and away from him instead though, she stopped herself in her tracks. The sun was glaring down on top of her and its heat wrapped around her face as if she held a hot towel there, smothering her, the waves enveloping her head completely, until she was almost stifled. She managed to catch her breath. Quite having taken leave of her senses, not to say her manners, she turned to join Paul again. She had been so rude to him. Had thought such dreadfully horrible things of him and what he might be capable of. He in return had shown her nothing but kindness, generosity, hospitality and now the depths of his feelings for her.

With a heavy heart, full of guilt, remorse even, she entered his home and sat back beside him again. Turning to face him this time, she looked at his eyes. They were shining, sparkling like a child's. He seemed nervous. She hadn't given him much hope so far. They sat there for a moment, saying nothing while both tried to make things right again between them. At long last he rose, smiled, the strain showing on his face and turned away from the scene. She stood and went to him to apologise but he was already halfway across towards his chickens and too lost in his own emotions to hear anything she had to say.

There were, naturally, other schools she could have tried to find work at, many of which were orphanages. She remembered one such orphanage in particular, where her heart had once more been filled with hope and inspiration. It was out in the depths of the jungle, far, far away from everything and everyone else. The buildings were just about as primitive as you could imagine, mud or clay walls and corrugated iron for a roof. Around the place were chickens, goats, the odd cow, dogs, kittens, all roaming or running freely amidst the children. At least, those children who were deemed too young to contribute to the work effort. Everyone else had something they needed to be getting on with to help keep the place ticking over. It seemed that was pretty much all they could expect from their meagre existence, here and in most places she had come across.

It was in the cities, in the capital, Mutabi, where there was any real evidence of wealth, if it could be called that. There at least could be found office buildings, commercial premises, consumer products, bars and even the occasional restaurant. Although, from previous trips there she recognised how deceiving things can be, how any essence of development was largely over-shadowed by the poverty and pestilence, disease and destruction which capped it as the clouds over Table Mountain, to the south.

On one visit to the orphanage known as Karpatee, meaning 'togetherness,' she had been invited to attend a presentation and thanksgiving of sorts. When she arrived with some other teachers from the boys' school, left deep down in the valley below Karpatee and out of sight here, she found herself overcome with joy. They had erected, somehow, an awning to provide shade for her in the scorching heat which had greeted them that afternoon and had for many days before. There was a table with a long bench for her and the others to watch the proceedings from, like royalty. In fact, in as many ways as they could, the people at the orphanage made their guests feel, not simply at home, as if that were not enough, but special too.

The children had organised a parade to start the proceedings, from the smallest to the tallest. All turned out in their beautiful traditional clothes, headdresses, the lot, they walked into the centre of their mock stage, turned to address their audience and then all moved to the side, save one. The prettiest little girl she had clapped eyes on, no more than six or seven years of age, began to shuffle her feet in time to the rhythmic clapping of her fellow orphans. The next thing she heard was the enchanting melody of the same girl singing what could only have been a song passed down from her ancestors. She wasn't able to recognise many of the words, though it was wonderful to the ear.

Looking to her side, one of her companions leant over and whispered a brief translation. The song was about a tiny bird that hadn't been noticed in its nest. When the other fledglings grew big and strong enough to leave their parents, the smallest went to try to join them, but she only got trampled on in all the excitement and hid beneath some twigs. The parents moved on too, leaving the poor, lonely fledgling to fend for itself. Until one night an owl spotted the baby bird and took it, meaning to have it for its supper. But, when the owl reached its own nest, which was a hollow in an old tree, the tiny bird clamped in the owl's beak, managed to sing the simplest and most delightful of songs the owl had ever heard. The tune was somehow amplified by the tree and so all the night creatures were able to hear it too. They crept out to listen further and the owl, glancing down at the animals before him, standing altogether like that, released the bird from its beak. As the tiny fledgling was released it was free once more, it took flight and flitted over the tilted heads of the animals on the ground beneath it, singing its wondrous song as it did so. The owl blinked at the sight and called out to the little bird, "you are very special." From now on this place shall be known as *Karpatee*. And so the name of the orphanage was given, or so the song went.

She thanked her translator and joined in with the applause with everyone else as the little orphan girl curtsied and ran to the side to join her friends. She had the most enormous smile on her face, as big, almost, as that of the girl soloist. She wiped a tear from her eye and waited to find out what else they planned to enthral her with.

She didn't have to wait long before a group of young girls skipped back to centre stage and got into position for a spectacular dance routine. Meanwhile, the boys were to each side of them, kneeling on the ground with a drum between their legs. Beating in time with each other as the girls hopped and twirled about, their hands on their hips, above their heads and chanting as one. It was a noisy, though enjoyable, performance. Everyone had smiles on their faces and there was applauding all round. The drumming seemed to come to an abrupt stop, a pause and then it would begin again, louder still and faster, faster, the girls keeping time with the rhythm, the audience clapping in keeping too. It was brilliant. She wanted to stand up, but kept herself from getting too carried away, although why she felt the need to come across as so conservative she had no idea. The smallest children from the orphanage who were dancing, joined hands and in unison they bent their backs forwards and over, tilted their heads down, hunched their shoulders up and down and then lifted their heads up to their audience and back again. This dance movement was repeated several times until one half of the girls circled off to the right, the other to the left. They joined up in the middle once more, but with the smallest child at the front, to the tallest at the rear. Then the first girl stepped forward and like a gymnast threw her hands out and down and flipped herself over and back onto her feet again. The second girl accomplished the same energetic feat and then each girl behind, true to form, flipped consequentially with such drive and confidence, culminating in a long horizontal line, and one perfect courtesy in unison. The drumming ceased. Marvellous! She was in awe of them. Brilliant. Pure brilliance.

She was certainly standing now, but then, not surprisingly, so was everyone else who was there to watch the show. Overcome, she was biting her lip to stop herself blubbing. Maybe she could adopt one or two or more of these children? She could help run the orphanage, forget about university and stay out here, give something back, leave a legacy, build another orphanage?

Some of the teachers were up and walking about, congratulating the children and staff. She found herself sort of coming to. She had virtually been in a trance with the music, the singing, the dancing, those cherubims. Now she was experiencing a reality check. If she truly wanted to help here she would need to get herself sorted first. That meant finishing her education back home, then she could secure a decent position which should make it easier for her to achieve such visions as working out here permanently, and making a difference. She was twenty-nine, still impressionable, full of ideas, dreams. She stood there and hoped, prayed even that whatever happened, what or whoever got in her way, tried to dissuade her she would keep that spark inside her, even if it was naivety.

It was during the prize giving that the shots were first heard. They rang out from a long way off at first, but that was just the beginning. There was more danger much closer to hand as men, camouflaged in their army kit, sprang out at them. They seemed to pounce from all directions, like a wolf pack that had followed a scent trail and ravenous now, had caught up with its prey. Brandishing weapons in the form of guns, machetes, knives, their hands even, they threw themselves at anyone in their path, eyes glaring, mouths in a grimace.

The children were in shock, some screaming, the older ones clutching the smallest and trying to run off into the shadows of the trees behind them. But they were only falling into the very hands of those aggressors who sought to harm them. Others were attempting to grab sticks and rocks to use to defend themselves, but they were no match for this band of rebels.

She guessed the men and noticeably even some women, may have broken off from the main army. Possibly it was lack of pay or no pay. Presumably, the government meant well, but they lacked provisions, the basics, money to satisfy the greedy pockets of every merciless, corrupt, useless official they felt compelled to keep on board with them.

This was the result. People were panic-stricken. There were blades, blood and skin flying all over the place. She saw horrors she didn't believe she would ever wipe from her mind. Teeth were scattered around the floor, scalps even. Why couldn't this be a nightmare and not the massacre she had found herself caught up in? She did see some of the staff and children get away. At least she prayed they had. They would get help, surely? Then these monsters would be caught and brought to justice. There was that word again, justice.

Nausea had kicked in now. Her head felt hot. Stumbling forwards, she fell onto her knees, her palms face down now on the ground under her. She looked at the blood that was dripping into the soil before her and tried to lift a hand to the gaping wound on the back of her head. She slumped forwards with the effort. Things were hard to see now. Her vision was blurred with the blood, the pain, the fear. Darkness was setting in.

There was a shoe to one side of her, she could just make out the owner's leg was still inside, cut off haphazardly below the knee. She noticed the laces were still tied. How bizarre that she should have noticed that. Then she saw more shoes, boots, two of them standing firm right in front of her. She blinked the blood out of her eyes in an effort to discover who was there, friend or foe. But she realised quickly these boots were army issue. In any case most of the orphans lived in sandals. How odd again that such detail should concern her now. Then he spoke.

"Sarah. Sarah, is it you? Sarah, it's going to be alright. I know a good doctor."

She knew that voice. Samuel. Not possible. No. Darkness.

"Sarah. Sarah. Come on now. I've brought you your tea. It's just as you like it, warm and milky and the nice new doctor is here to see how you are getting on now."

She looked up. Turned her head with difficulty to either side of her to the men and women sitting with her. One or two smiled slightly, another was staring out of a window that looked onto a lake with a statue standing before it. She recognised it as Venus. The voice came again. This time addressing the doctor.

"Sarah has been with us for quite some time now. Haven't you, Sarah?"

She didn't respond.

"She has some issues with memory loss and mobility difficulties, but then you would have read the notes already. These are her friends, aren't they Sarah?"

Still no reply.

"Let me introduce you to them, doctor. This is James, Andrew, Matthew, Charles and Louise but Sarah has her own names for us."

The doctor only nodded a gesture of interest, cupping his chin with thumb and forefinger.

"Yes. She seems to prefer to use the names Scott, Ben, Michael and Tom. Louise here, apparently, is Tom and Michael's sister, Amanda. You will be well informed I'm sure,

Sarah had a troubled past. Horrible, shocking. She rarely speaks, though the therapy and drug medication here may be exacerbating that."

"And what does she call you?" asked the doctor.

"Me? Oh, I'm Samuel. Isn't that right Sarah?"

Sarah gave no reply.

"Now come on doctor, we have taken up far too much of your time already. Let me walk you through to the other areas of the home here. I'm certain you will be impressed with the facilities we have been blessed with. All courtesy of Lottery funding and a generous gesture from an unknown philanthropist. Rumour has it he or she has contacts with a rebel faction somewhere in Africa. What exciting times we live in doctor. One has to be so grateful for any help one can get these days, wouldn't you agree?"

"Actually, that brings us around very aptly to the other reason for my visit," added the doctor.

"Oh yes?"

"Fund raising."

"Fund raising. Where would we be without the help of well-wishers, hey?"

"Quite. Well, as you may or may not be aware, the Board and I have decided this Summer Fayre should be given our biggest effort yet. With a great deal of persuasion, plus a little coercion if I'm being honest with you, we hope to produce a spectacular afternoon's fun and entertainment."

"That is wonderful news, doctor. What sort of entertainment did you have planned?"

"Oh, you know, the usual, plus a vintage carousel. Shire horse display, circus performers, even a bearded lady."

"It does sound terribly grand and exciting. Call in a few favours did we?"

"Well, needs must and all that. You know how it is. Anything for a good cause, what."

The days and weeks seemed to fly by with all the organising there needed to be done. Finally, the afternoon of the Fayre arrived to everyone's great excitement and jubilation. The hospital grounds were carpeted with hoards of colourful looking people enjoying the fine weather. All of them ready to make the most of the wonderful displays about them.

Naturally, those hospital residents who were able to join in the day's activities did so with great glee and gusto. Feeling the break away from their usual existence so uplifting, some barely seemed to cease smiling and laughing all day long.

For Sarah it was the carousel. Not since she was a young child had she travelled on one of those magnificent rides. She chose her favourite, a horse, then held tight to the golden pole that took her up, then down like a giant piece of golden candy, sliding through her palms. She let her head fall back a little with the sheer pleasure of it all. Forgetting the pain she constantly endured from the attack at the orphanage, for just a few moments. Then, sitting up straight again, she turned her face to look out at the crowd about the carousel. There was a mixture of children of varying ages, some with their parents, a few older ones, seemingly without. The ride came round again. She spotted candyfloss, toffee apples, coconuts, balloons, enormous soft toy giraffes, pandas and gorillas. It was all there. She smiled contentedly, sitting deep into the saddle.

When all at once she sat bolt upright. The ride carried on. There he was again, a man she recognised, a man from long, long ago. Then he was gone. Again the carousel turned her to him again and it was then that she saw he was holding something to her. Gone. There it was, a small box open presumably, because she caught a glimpse of something inside. No more then, there, the sun was gleaming on him and the open box now and she saw and then she knew. The face was one who had captured her heart as a young inexperienced girl. But a boy himself then, they had shared a love for horses and a summer together she had never forgotten. In the palm of his hand he held out a ring that through tears of joy was almost winking at her. But for the attack and everything she would have remembered his name. The horses climbed with the thoughts in her head, desperate to recall. That was when he saved her once more.

"It's James," he called out. "Marry me?"

Of course, she said to herself. The carousel was slowing now, round it came, slower and slower still, then stopped.

"Of course," she said. "James."